# THE WHITE LADY

***Paul Halter books from LRI:***
The Lord of Misrule (2010)
The Fourth Door (2011)
The Seven Wonders of Crime (2011)
The Demon of Dartmoor (2012)
The Seventh Hypothesis (2012)
The Tiger's Head (2013)
The Crimson Fog (2013)
The Night of the Wolf collection (2013)
The Invisible Circle (2014)
The Picture from the Past (2014)
The Phantom Passage (2015)
Death Invites You (2016)
The Vampire Tree (2016)
The Madman's Room (2017)
The Man Who Loved Clouds (2018)
The Gold Watch (2019)
The Helm of Hades collection (2019)

***Other impossible crime books from LRI:***
The Riddle of Monte Verita (Jean-Paul Török) 2012
The Killing Needle (Henry Cauvin) 2014
The Derek Smith Omnibus (Derek Smith) 2014
The House That Kills (Noel Vindry) 2015
The Decagon House Murders (Yukito Ayatsuji) 2015
Hard Cheese (Ulf Durling) 2015
The Moai Island Puzzle (Alice Arisugawa) 2016
The Howling Beast (Noel Vindry) 2016
Death in the Dark (Stacey Bishop) 2017
The Ginza Ghost collection (Keikichi Osaka) 2017
Death in the House of Rain (Szu-Yen Lin) 2017
The Double Alibi (Noel Vindry) 2018
The 8 Mansion Murders (Takemaru Abiko) 2018
The Seventh Guest (Gaston Boca) 2018
The Flying Boat Mystery (Franco Vailati) 2019
Death out of Nowhere (Alexis Gensoul & Charles Garnier) 2020
The Red Locked Room collection (Tetsuya Ayukawa) 2020

***Bibliographies***
Locked Room Murders Second Edition, Revised 2018
Locked Room Murders Supplement 2019

Visit our website at www.mylri.com or
www.lockedroominternational.com

# THE WHITE LADY

*Paul Halter*

*Translated by John Pugmire*

# The White Lady

This book is a work of fiction. The characters, incidents, and dialogue are drawn from the author's imagination and are not to be construed as real. Any resemblance to actual events or persons, living or dead, is entirely coincidental.

Original French title *Le Mystère de la Dame Blanche*.
Copyright © Paul Halter 2020.
THE WHITE LADY
English translation copyright © by John Pugmire 2020.

All rights reserved. No part of this book may be used or reproduced in any manner whatsoever without written permission except in the case of brief quotations embodied in critical articles and reviews.

Cover design by Joseph Gérard

For information, contact: pugmire1@yahoo.com

FIRST AMERICAN EDITION
Library of Congress Cataloguing-in-Publication Data
Halter, Paul
[*Le Mystère de la Dame Blanche* English]
The White Lady / Paul Halter
Translated from the French by John Pugmire

*The eye was in the tomb and regarded Cain*
Victor Hugo, The Legend of the Ages II « The Conscience »

## Prologue

What is Death?

An abstract notion? Or something concrete, with form and colour?

Death in colour—doesn't that sound poetic?

I believe red fits it like a glove. The Red Death, as in the plague epidemics... Or the black of grieving and funeral ceremonies. Black like the deepest darkness, absolute chaos, nothing.

And blue, in a way. Don't they talk about "a blue funk"? Maybe because blue is the coldest colour?

The coldest? That's white. Definitely white. Dazzling white! White death, the purest and most inevitable, that which comes from the iciest regions of the world, the outer edges of the universe. The terrifying cold which seizes you when the time comes. And freezes you forever....

Sometimes we imagine death as a skeleton holding a scythe. The Grim Reaper... Children draw it as a nasty crocodile with greedy yellow eyes, or as a black wolf with pointed ears and enormous blood-red eyes....

But some manifestations are subtler and stranger... even impressions of false gaiety. Take the example of the clown, the very symbol of laughter. But would he make you laugh if he rang your doorbell at midnight on a glacial winter night, and you came face to face with a motionless figure on your doorstep?

The same goes for an egg-timer, the most banal of objects, used in the kitchen or in some games. But to discover one on your kitchen table, just after you've woken up, slowly dispensing its grains of sand... like time running out before your inevitable end.

Yes, Death likes to play with us, presenting many facets, including the least expected and the most deceptive....

The approach of a pack of wolves in an isolated clearing. What could be more terrifying? Even the presence of a slender and innocent creature amongst the pack, such as a young girl dressed in white, would change nothing. The impression of menace would stay the same. And if the wolves were to withdraw and the delicate apparition were to walk slowly towards you, the effect would be even more terrifying...

Even so, there's no more striking contrast than that of the wild beast and the innocent young girl with the angelic face. Truth be told, Death knows how to make itself recognised, whatever its mask, and transmit its message to you. Without saying a word, it can make you understand that the moment has come for you to follow it....

The legend of the White Ladies is a perfect illustration.

The famous White Ladies... sometimes washerwomen, sometimes sirens, sometimes ghosts of women betrayed or abandoned, and often vengeful.

It's not known of which kind is the one that has haunted Buckworth for centuries. But what is certain is that her appearance is always a bad omen.

I'd like to talk to you about her, for I know her well.

I believe I know her evil designs, the reason for her existence, her dark acts, her regular visits in defiance of time or any material obstacle.

Whether you revere her, fear her, or hate her, no one can stop her. She is elusive and relentless.

You might see her from afar in her restless wanderings, in an alleyway, a clearing in a forest or by a pond. If that happens, do nothing. Only look at her briefly. Or better yet, lower your eyes. Inquisitive looks could upset her, as if you were taking pleasure in the misfortunes of her life on earth.

But if she approaches, if she comes towards you, be aware that there's nothing you can do. Attempting to flee is futile, and you couldn't anyway. You would be hypnotised by her angelic smile, her unfathomable regard, fascinated by the purity of her white silhouette, and petrified by the increasing cold invading you....

A glacial cold, the kind that freezes rivers and everything else down here. Her arm will be raised slowly towards you, her white hand will be placed on your heart, and you will experience cracks in your chest like fissures in a glacier....

1

**Memories of India**

*September 13, 1924*

The local train rattled monotonously as it traversed the English countryside. It was already well into the afternoon, but the sun still hadn't shown its face. Margot Peel looked disinterestedly at the young woman asleep on the seat opposite, near the window. A small crocodile-skin suitcase was perched on the overhead rack above her. Margot didn't attach any particular importance to it at that moment. The unknown woman's head was thrown back, her face was covered by a cascade of black ringlets, and her hands had been brought up under her chin. In fact, only her ankles, slender and beautifully turned, were visible, betraying the grace and elegance of their owner. Margot shot a glance at her own. They were nothing to be ashamed of, any more than the rest of her person or her face, which she could see reflected in the mirror above the seat opposite. It was that of a young woman approaching thirty, with regular features framed by chestnut hair. Her complexion seemed to her to be too pale and her lips too thin. As for her large eyes, of different colours—for one was more turquoise than blue—they gave an impression of vagueness which reflected only too well her personality, that of someone tired of fighting and resigned to her fate. That was what was altering her appearance, she thought. A pretty enough girl, but no more than that. What if she were to wear more showy clothes? Like the vivid red coat of the girl asleep opposite, which stood out against the dreary countryside rolling past the window?

No, she thought, after sober reflection. In fact, she had once tried it, to no effect. Muted colours were more suited to her personality than exuberant ones. Sitting next to her, slumped in the corner nearest the door, John had also succumbed to the relentless rhythm of the train. She looked at him for a moment, as tears started to well in her eyes. She opened her handbag to reveal a faded pink envelope. It contained the last letter from her sister, which she had read and re-read, and which had resulted in her and John finding themselves at Paddington Station half-an-hour earlier, bags packed, to travel to Buckworth, the village where she was born. There was another letter, sent by the civil service two months earlier, which had given her the shock of her life, and which she had never let out of her sight since.

Margot closed her tear-filled eyes and thought of the recent past, when she had been invited to dinner by the dashing William at one of London's best restaurants. The sparkling silver, the animated conversation, William's dazzling smile, the beautiful ring... It was as if it were yesterday. But then time went further backwards, to the distant past when she was a happy and innocent young girl, just like her sister Ann, two years her junior. Both were well looked after in the loving presence of their mother and the comforting presence of their father, Sir Matthew Richards, the last offspring of the richest family in the county. The setting for those happy days was Buckworth Manor, the family residence set in the middle of a beautiful property on the outskirts of the village. She and Ann were undoubtedly the most blessed children in the area. At the end of the Great War, when she was twenty-three years old, she had accompanied her father to India, whilst Ann and her mother had preferred to wait for them in the comfort of the familial home. Matthew Richards had gone there on business, because he was not one to rest on his laurels and watch the slow decline of the family inheritance. He had ventured successfully into financial speculation and the commerce of precious stones. Together with a partner, he controlled a sapphire mine near the northern Indian border. Hence the reason for the voyage, which was to last no more than six months. Sir Matthew liked to control things personally and keep them close to his chest. But controlling the sentiments of a twenty-three-year-old girl was quite another matter....

During one of the many balls, Margot had met a seductive major in the Indian army, who had won her heart. Unfortunately, her father had viewed the budding romance with a different eye. He felt strongly that she merited more than a humble military man, and told her so in no uncertain terms. That was their first altercation, recalled Margot. He who had always cherished her, perhaps even more than her sister, was suddenly transformed into a ferocious tiger, like the one whose head decorated the walls of their bungalow. Faced with such brute force, she could only resort to guile. She pretended to surrender. Then one day, as he returned from a long field trip, she presented him with a *fait accompli*: his darling daughter was now a married woman. And she added mischievously that he didn't need to look far to find the origin of her independent character. This last remark undoubtedly tempered his reaction, but he nevertheless informed her that he would ensure that the young couple were indeed independent and she should pack her bags. That was in mid-May of 1919. At the end of that month, her husband was dispatched with the rest of his regiment to the Afghan border, to put down a major rebellion.

A few days later, she was summoned to identify the body of her husband, as the result of a veritable butchery, a memory which would haunt her for life. Three weeks after getting married, she found herself a widow, alone and lost.

Despite her desperate situation, she had not been able to bring herself to ask her father for help. Another military man, Patrick, himself a survivor of the terrible events, had taken care of her. He was a friend of her husband who resembled him physically and understood her situation. He had offered her help, without asking for anything in return. After several weeks, during which their friendship had blossomed, they had become lovers. Patrick was a charming and attentive companion who had managed to make her forget her grief. But after a few months of happy union he had suddenly disappeared from her life. She had been led to understand that he had been assigned to a reconnaissance mission from which no one had returned. After that second painful existence, she had vowed never to be involved with a soldier again. And she had kept her word. Her next companion had been a native, a handsome Indian of the same age, acting as an interpreter for the army. Their passion had only lasted a short while. Their idyll had been damned from the start and they were shunned from all sides. Her few English friends had regarded her as less than nothing from then on, and her lover had suffered the wrath of his family, to the point of being severely beaten. They could have found salvation by fleeing, but to where? To another place, to be plunged into the same torment, or worse?

A lump came into Margot's throat as she recalled the night they had bid each other goodbye, their farewell kiss just as passionate as their first. There were too many obstacles on their path to happiness, and neither of them had the strength to surmount them. Meanwhile, her father had returned home and she had learnt of the death of her mother, who had long suffered from a pulmonary disease. She had decided to return to England. The misery of India, its suffocating climate, her series of personal disasters, her restless wanderings... she could no longer stay. She had felt she had to leave.

She had been happy to see her sister Ann, who had married in the meantime, and her father, who had decided to bury the hatchet. He had welcomed her warmly, but not without the occasional reminder of "the cost of independence." Nevertheless, despite the comfort of the family home, she had decided to move to London, accepting the post of manageress of a jewellery store owned by her father—for she had made it a point of honour to refuse any direct help. She vowed to dedicate herself entirely to her work, to the exclusion of any romantic relationship, in view of all her past suffering. Several years passed without event until she became friendly with William, the assistant manager of her local bank. A purely platonic relationship at first, but steady. He invited her regularly to dinner and she cherished those moments, which were in fact her only noticeable contact with society. She sensed that William had strong feelings towards her, but did not press his case, for fear of breaking their fragile bond. But, in view of her own growing feelings, there was little risk of that.

One evening, however, as they met for their weekly rendezvous, he took the plunge and presented her with a beautiful emerald ring. He was so nervous he failed to notice her wary expression.

'I know that this might appear offensive, Margot,' he had said, 'but I didn't purchase it from your boutique because I wanted to surprise you... That said, it's not without value. The emerald is from Colombia, from the Muzo mine, the best in the world....'

'I know,' she had replied, choking back her anguish.

'Of course. What was I thinking? I hope you'll forgive my careless mistake. It was due to my emotion. I so much wanted to surprise you because—.'

'No, William, don't say any more, I beg of you.'

After a weighty silence, he continued:

'I love you, Margot. It's as simple as that... and I thought that only an emerald from Muzo was worthy of you, because since the very first day I set eyes on you...'

'I can't accept, William.'

'So you... you don't...'

As pale as death, she had replied:

'Yes. I love you more and more, as you must realise. But...'

'Then what's the problem?' he asked, removing his glasses and staring into her eyes.

That was the moment she had lowered her eyes and burst into tears. Then, rummaging in her handbag, she had produced a letter, which she had placed on the table.

'This is the problem. Read it yourself and you'll understand... Understand that I am full of happiness and grief at the same time.'

'Happiness and grief?' he asked in astonishment. 'How is that possible? It has to be one or the other.'

'Read it, I beg you.'

She had watched her companion's features pale as he was reading. When he had finished, he had wiped his brow and stammered, his eyes wide open:

'John Peel... your late husband... is still alive.'

2

## Memories of Africa

'I received the letter this morning,' Margot had said, sighing, 'and I have to see him tomorrow.'

'Do... do you still love him?'

'I don't know what I feel, William... Please try to understand. First of all I must see him... But whatever shape he's in, and whatever my feelings for you may be, I fear I won't be able to bring myself to abandon him...'

The next day, when she was face to face with her husband, whom she had only known for a few weeks and had not seen for five years, the shock was so intense that she fainted, even though she had been warned that he had changed considerably because of what had happened to him. The John Peel that she had known was a mere shadow of his former self. He had aged almost beyond recognition, his hair had turned ashen, and the left side of his face was scarred from badly-healed wounds. His memory, moreover, had been severely affected so that the only clear recollections were of the nightmare he had endured for several years. He had, in fact, been captured by the rebels, who had treated him like a slave, beating him and whipping him at the slightest sign of resistance. After three infernal years, he had managed to escape and find refuge in a Kashmiri village. The inhabitants had taken pity on him and taken care of him to the best of their ability, but it had taken months before he had recovered sufficiently to rejoin the nearest garrison. Margot's misidentification of a severely disfigured body as her husband's was due to his helmet having been found nearby.

Yet, no matter how painful her memories, Margot had discovered that she still loved him as much as in their first days. His ardent look, full of suppressed joy, like a dog reunited with its master, had touched her to her very core. For several long minutes, they had sat clutching each other, crying as if their hearts would break....

Then, day by day, they had shared their histories with each other, a little at a time. There had, of course, been many gaps in John's, whose state of health had nevertheless visibly continued to improve. The only after-effects had been the bad memories, the violent headaches and the scars to his face. The doctor treating him had been optimistic about his chances of a full recovery. And so, slowly, their life as a couple had risen from the ashes.

Turning to look at her husband, still asleep in the corner seat, despite the jolting of the train, Margot wondered tenderly: *If we hadn't had such suffering, would we have been as happy as we are today? Without all that, would we have been just another long-married couple looking daggers at each other?*

About a month after they had found each other, Margot had felt that she had had more than her fair share of misfortune, and that she was close to leading as peaceful a life as when she was a child. That was when she had received the first letter from her sister....

*My dearest Margot,*

*As I suspect that father has failed to tell you the news, it falls to me, at the risk of upsetting you at a time you don't need it. I hope all is going well for you and John, and that he's recovering from his horrible ordeal.*

*To begin at the beginning, about a month ago father hired a full-time secretary, even though I was already doing the work for him. Needless to say, she is young and very pretty! You probably don't know as much about the subject as I do, but even you know that father has always been a womaniser, even before mother died. I wouldn't be surprised if some day someone knocked on the door to announce that they were my brother or my sister! (On top of all the village gossip, I know for a fact that he had an affair with someone of dubious character, but physically attractive and young, of course.)*

*The new secretary, whose name is Vivian, settled in very quickly and soon made herself indispensable to our dear father, whose seventy years have not made him any less susceptible to female charm. Even so... a more than forty-year age difference! I tried to convince myself it was just an old man's folly, as did Peter and Esther, but yesterday at dinner, he announced that he and Vivian had just tied the knot! Just like that, with no warning! I thought that such things only happened in cheap paperbacks.*

*So now we have a new mother, younger than both of us. Needless to say, we're not fooled. The fair Vivian didn't marry father just for his beautiful eyes. She's a vulgar schemer whose plan is obvious to everyone, except father, of course. So that's the situation, dear sister of mine. I'll keep you posted, of course.*

Her second letter had come the week before. Margot took it out of her bag to read it again, even though she knew its content almost by heart.

*Help, Margot dear! The bitch has literally bewitched father! She now does whatever she wants, she runs everything. She's clever about it, always playing the innocent and making "suggestions"... and father makes sure her every wish is granted. Esther and I have been reduced to maidservants. I beg you, come and help us. You're the only one with any influence over father. Spend some time with us here. Come with John. We need you to fight this cunning invader, and most of all, take the wool from over father's eyes. I'm sure he would be delighted to have you and John stay with us for a few weeks. From where he is, with his head stuck in the clouds, he thinks everything is fine and the whole family should be there to celebrate his birthday.*

'Are you reading that letter again, darling?'
Margot turned to her husband, who was smiling at her through a barely suppressed yawn.
'Yes,' she sighed, 'I can't help it.'
'But we can't turn back, can we? The die is cast! And we're off to new adventures.'
'New adventures,' repeated Margot, before running through a list of her trials and tribulations over the last few years.
John Peel listened in silence as she reeled off the list.
'I thought I'd suffered enough,' she concluded. 'And now my own father has lost his head to a vulgar adventurist. It will be almost more than I can do, not to jump down her throat when we're introduced... I'm not even thirty, yet I feel so old, so weary of life.'
'You're not the only one, madam.'
Margot turned to look at the unknown woman in the red coat who, like John, had just woken up. Goodness! She'd completely forgotten

about her and had poured out her soul in front of her!

The olive-complexioned young woman was quite beautiful. Her large, dark eyes regarded her travelling companions with a grave, mysterious expression.

'Please excuse me, madam,' stammered Margot. 'I thought you were asleep. Rest assured, I'm not in the habit of unburdening myself in front of others.'

The young woman shrugged her shoulders nonchalantly.

'I, too, have had my fair share of misery, and I know it sometimes helps to talk about it. Unfortunately, my life has been so extraordinary that people generally don't believe me.'

There was an awkward silence. As the woman looked up at her small suitcase, John made a discreet sign to his wife, who had been about to answer.

'We would be happy to be the judge of that, madam,' he said with an amiable smile. 'That would place us on equal footing when it came to confessions.'

After another silence, the young woman ran a hand gracefully through her black locks, and started to tell her story:

'It was in Africa and I was barely twenty years old. I'll skip the circumstances that had taken me there; suffice to say that my companion had abandoned me and I found myself in a small village surrounded by natives. I don't know whether I was really in love with the tall, handsome fellow I had ended up marrying—according to local custom, that is. But I do know that he was very proud of me, and tried very hard to make me happy. One bright day, Moussa—that was his name—had left our hut, suitcase in hand, announcing in his deep voice that we were henceforth very rich. Without going into details, he asked me to get ready and join him to leave the village. He took me down to the river, to a dugout canoe on the bank.'

'I remember as if it were yesterday... It was a magnificent day, with the water sparkling in the sunlight. Everything seemed to be going well as we started to load our luggage. Then suddenly an individual dressed in panther skin emerged out of the blue to push us aside, jump into the canoe and row rapidly away. "The suitcase!" shouted Moussa, as he dived into the river to pursue the fugitive. But around him in the river, what had seemed to be logs started to move, converging on him. Shortly afterwards he disappeared in a huge pool of blood, torn to pieces by crocodiles. In just a few seconds I had lost everything: my husband, everything we owned, and the suitcase supposed to contain a small fortune. I'll skip over the details of the nightmare which followed.

'A few days later, in a nearby market, imagine my surprise to discover the suitcase in a shop for tourists. It was the very same, I would have recognised it anywhere! The owner told me he had bought it just recently, from a seller whose description matched that of the fugitive thief. As I tried to examine it more closely, he warned me against opening it, telling me it was not meant for that. I recognised the complicated knots of string around the handle and the locks as the work of Moussa. "Opening it brings bad luck," he had warned me. "It has to be sold the way it is." The price the shop owner was asking was well above my means. What surprised me most of all was that the thief seemed not to have had the elementary curiosity to open it, perhaps because of the mysterious curse. Nevertheless, I had made my decision. On leaving the shop, I picked a quarrel with a passing young black man, and in the ensuing tumult I grabbed the suitcase and ran off with it.'

She stopped and shook her head, as if mocking herself. Then she continued:

'In addition to being foolhardy, I was stupid. Because after all that had happened, I couldn't bring myself to open it. I'm not superstitious, far from it, but in Africa things are different... The people, the poverty, the overpowering heat... One submits against one's will. It's difficult to understand that, here in England.'

'Oh, I understand very well, madam,' sighed Margot. 'And perhaps more than you think.'

'Well then, you're ready for the next part. Shortly afterwards, I made the acquaintance of a young Frenchman, an army deserter who had been in hiding. He was quite dashing, even so, and one night, when we were drunk, I'd told him about my mysterious suitcase. By the next morning, he had disappeared, and the suitcase with him. But it didn't bring him luck. He was found mortally beaten at the place where he usually stored his loot. Luckily for me, he'd given the suitcase and some personal effects to a friend beforehand. I had to pay him with my body to get it back.'

She pulled a face and continued quickly:

'Which I would have refused to do normally, but nothing is normal there, as I said... In addition to the suitcase, the man had had the decency to let me have a little money from the deceased's funds.'

'And the suitcase... was it still intact?' asked John anxiously.

'Yes, I decided to wait for my return to Europe before opening it. I felt that nothing bad could befall me there. Weeks and months passed. I began to realise I had an effect on men. In Cairo, I met and married a rich Englishman, to the great disappointment of an even richer Egyptian, who refused to give up. Shortly after the marriage, he succeeded in provoking my husband into a duel... and I found myself a widow once more. At that point, I decided I was finished with marriage, even though my husband's assassin kept pressing me. I had the cunning inspiration to mention the mysterious suitcase to him during a Nile crossing. The next morning I could see that the string of knots were still there, but had been disturbed. On weighing it, I reassured myself that the contents were still there. My Egyptian suitor, however, was not. They found his body on the banks of the Nile, in a patch of papyrus, drowned. Was it accident or suicide? The inquest was unable to determine.

'After other disappointments, which are irrelevant, I managed to reach France and then England. Now, believe it or not, I decided to open it last night.'

In the suffocating silence that followed, Margot nodded in the direction of the small suitcase on the rack opposite, and asked:

'Is that the one?'

'The very same,' said the other with a Giaconda smile. 'Would you like to know what's inside?'

'Very much so,' said John. 'It would be cruel not to do so now.'

The young woman's smile widened:

'Very well. To put it simply: *everything I've told you is rubbish!*'

To the astonishment of her audience, she threw her head back and roared with laughter for what seemed an interminable time. She eventually calmed down and added:

'Please forgive my little joke, but I think it was warranted after all the attacks on my person. Allow me to introduce myself. I'm Vivian Richards, your father's new bride, my dear Margot. Or, if you prefer, your new mother....'

3

**The White Lady**

In the grand salon of Buckworth Manor, Peter Corsham laughed heartily after having heard Margot's account of the famous suitcase. A slender man in his thirties with a fine moustache, he had a distinguished yet relaxed air about him, and an irresistible dimpled smile that had captivated Ann. That was then—at the time they met, before they became man and wife—for at the moment she was eyeing him severely, offended as she was by his hilarity.

'I don't see what's so funny Peter,' she said through gritted teeth. 'It's yet more proof of her incredible effrontery.'

'Perhaps, darling, but she's not lacking in resourcefulness.'

'That was never in doubt,' retorted Ann, still shaking with anger, her red cheeks contrasting with her naturally pale complexion.

Ann Corsham was a smaller version of her sister, thinner and more angular. With her blonde locks swept up in a hairnet and her fine features and pale blue eyes, she resembled a Nordic warrior, especially when she was contradicted.

'In fact, darling,' Peter replied, 'she may be more subtle than I had thought.' Turning to John Peel, he continued. 'Don't you agree she could have reacted otherwise, Major, after all the unflattering comments she'd been forced to listen to?'

'Quite true,' agreed the major, smilingly ensconced in an armchair. 'She had every right to be upset. Don't you think so, darling?'

Margot nodded in agreement:

'Yes, and I regret my mistake. I was ashamed, upset and amused, all at the same time... Anyway, it's all behind us, and we arrived here without any gnashing of teeth.'

'Ah, she's very astute!' grumbled Ann. 'She's in a league of her own when it comes to manipulating people by batting her eyelashes.'

'You have to admit she's a fine-looking filly,' observed John. 'But I wonder... with her olive complexion and black hair, is she really English?'

'Her origins remain a mystery,' replied Ann. 'She doesn't talk much about it, and when she does it's in a mixture of snatches of conversation interspersed with jokes, all in an incoherent jumble. It wouldn't surprise me to learn that there's something to her joke about her African wanderings.'

'The suitcase mystery,' mocked Peter. 'That would make a good title for a book.'

'That's enough for the time being,' announced Ann. 'John and Margot, you could probably use some rest. I'll have your bags sent up.'

Margot remained silent, looking around the room, bringing back memories. The familiar walls and furniture, this place where she had spent such a happy childhood... Nothing seemed to have changed. The last time she had seen Ann and Peter was when they had come to London to greet John on his miraculous return. Father had not been with them.

As they had passed through the entrance and crossed the park half-an-hour earlier, she had already started to wonder whether this return to her roots was wise. But John had seemed only too happy to be there, as did Vivian. Even so....

'Margot, are you with us?' asked Ann testily. 'What are you thinking about?'

'Nothing... I was just telling myself... But where's father? I thought he would have come to meet us.'

After the pendulum clock had struck half-past four, Ann replied:

'I don't believe he'll be long now. He's resting, as he's been doing every afternoon since... That's right, I haven't told you yet. You know he's always had an iron constitution, Margot, and made it a point to avoid doctors. But since last year, he's started to have heart problems. First one, then another, then a third, which really frightened us. That time the doctors were firm: avoid sustained activity and emotional stress, and force yourself to rest as much as possible, to avoid a premature appointment with St. Peter. For our part, we were to be careful not to contradict him or make him angry... Instructions cleverly enforced by a certain party, if you get my meaning. In other words, put up with everything without saying a word. Have you a better grasp of the problem now, sister dear?'

'None of which prevented him from marrying a high-spirited

creature,' said Peter ironically, serving himself another whisky. 'But who are we to point it out?'

A footstep on the stairs caused all their heads to turn. Then the door opened, to reveal the lord of the manor himself.

Tall, and with a proud bearing, Sir Matthew Richards was still a handsome man. He welcomed the newcomers warmly.

'The house is all yours, my children, and for as long as you like. Margot, surely you could have come to visit a little more often? As for you, John, please know that I am sincerely delighted to see you again, after your "resurrection." I hope that you'll forgive me not having been very conciliatory at one point, because... anyway, you understood. What you endured in the Afghan mountains commands the utmost respect, consideration, and, above all, my sincerest sympathy. Welcome to the family. I'm proud to have a son-in-law like you, who has done so much for your country. And the same goes for you, my darling Vivian, I assume?'

'Of course,' purred the young Lady Richards, her eyes sparkling with amusement. 'I can't wait to hear more about your exploits.'

Shortly thereafter, Peter invited John to take a tour of the park. After lighting a cigarette, he observed:

'I think you're in all right with the old man, John. And with the princess as well. You're in luck. Between you and me, sometimes it can be daggers drawn. Nothing serious, you understand, but sometimes she doesn't appreciate my jokes... particularly those about her privileged status. Otherwise, what did you think of her?'

Major John Peel rubbed his scarred cheek reflexively before replying:

'A very pretty woman... I can understand how she was able to turn your father-in-law's head.'

'Quite so. But what about the rest? Do you think the passion is reciprocated?'

'What I can tell you is that I've seen dozens of mature officers in similar circumstances, and in several cases the girls seemed to be equally smitten.'

'Could it be the attraction of the uniform?'

'Perhaps.'

'Or the bank account?'

'I don't think it's always so cut-and-dried. There's a lot of ground between grand passion and warm friendship.'

Peter ground his cigarette stub on the gravel path.

'I see. She's conquered you as well, old boy!'

The major's smile emphasised his scars.

'As I said, she's extremely pretty.'

'I fear you haven't had much experience with women. Which is understandable, given your long exile in the hands of those savage rebels.'

'I admit it. After I left this "sceptr'd isle," war was my principal mistress. What about you?'

'Let's just say I've enough experience to know what may lie behind a fresh young face. I'm not talking about Ann, of course. At the beginning, when Vivian started here as a simple secretary, I found her to be very nice, and I welcomed her bringing a touch of freshness inside these old walls. But afterwards, little by little....' He banged his fist into his palm. 'Surely it's not natural for a young filly like that to suddenly fall for an old man?'

Still smiling, John Peel replied:

'I'm not an idiot, believe me. The mountain air didn't completely soften my brain.'

A similar discussion was under way between the two sisters, in a small salon on the upper floor. The twilight threw a growing shadow into the unlit room.

'Frankly, Ann, it's too soon for me to form an idea about her,' sighed Margot, 'even if I do have confidence in your judgment. And if you are right, what then? Could we oppose our father's wishes? Go against his choice? What exactly do you want from me?'

'It's very simple. You have to help me open his eyes. He doesn't listen to me, or to Peter either. He already tried, but was quickly sent packing. With typical male condescendence, father retorted that he was only speaking out of jealousy. I was upset for him, and for me too, incidentally. As if I, his own daughter, were now to be eclipsed by that little bitch. And, speaking of father's wishes, you've hit a nerve, Margot: father called in his solicitor a couple of weeks ago to change his will. He didn't say anything to me, but it's not hard to guess in which sense.'

'Are you sure?'

'Yes, because I happened to get a glimpse of the old one, torn up in the waste-paper basket. And there were names other than yours and mine on it. Amongst them being young Seagrave, the washerwoman's daughter. Do you remember her?'

'Lethia? Of course. We used to play with her.'

'Well, it looks as though father has been her playmate recently... She's always been a bit weird, a bit of a wild child, always hanging about with animals. And over the last few years, after the death of her mother, she hasn't got any better. She's pretty well a recluse in her own house. Rumours abound, and nobody knows how she makes her living. Possibly through her fortune-telling talents, which are formidable according to father, who visited her a lot prior to his marriage. At least, that's what he says. I'm willing to bet there were other, less admirable, motives, and her name on the old will merely confirms my suspicions.'

Margot gave a deep sigh:

'He's always been a womaniser.'

'Yes,' agreed Ann, with a bitter smile. 'I don't know whether the pretty clairvoyant predicted that he would soon meet the woman of his life, but in any case she was soon supplanted by a more gifted magician than herself, one who succeeded in placing the ring on our father's finger and doubtless replacing her name in his will.'

'As I recall, Lethia was never a bad girl. Weird, maybe, but gentle and always looking after injured animals.'

'That's right. She's clearly more naïve and credulous than wicked... She's not the one to blame, it was father, who completely lost his head.'

There was a knock on the door and Esther appeared in the doorway.

'Dinner will be served in ten minutes,' she announced in a bored voice, before retiring.

Esther, good old Esther, thought Margot. She never changes, or only a little. Despite her sixty years, she had conserved her figure, and her beautiful Eurasian features. She had been their governess for as long back as she could remember.

'I know what you're thinking, sister dear,' declared Ann in the growing darkness. 'Esther, the loyal Esther... our second mother, so to speak... After our real mother's death—you weren't there, of course

—I wondered whether father wouldn't compensate her for her loyal service. But no. For him, Esther was part of the furniture. He didn't even see her.'

'Did you mean... marry her?'

'Yes, and I believe, had he done so, it would have been one of the best decisions he had ever made.'

'And Esther, how did she react? I mean, to the arrival of Vivian?'

'Always the same. Impassive, measured, correct, never a word out of place, but never obsequious... But I can imagine what lies behind her dark eyes, as she watches Vivian undress... She must be thinking the same thing as us. Well, shall we throw ourselves in the ring?'

\*\*\*

The next few days passed without incident. The country air seemed to have a beneficial effect on Major John Peel, who was starting to think about his professional future. His father-in-law, with whom he got on well, told him not to worry and he would take care of it, just as he had done for Peter. The latter was now the director of an insurance company in the City and enjoyed privileged hours, only going to London two or three days a week, just like Margot. Margot, who could be frequently seen in discussions with her sister. Peter and John frequently challenged each other in the billiard room, or at bridge in the company of the three young women of the house. Calm reigned in the vast ancestral home, until the following Saturday night....

Shortly after midnight, Esther was awakened by footsteps in the upstairs corridor, where all the bedrooms were located. As she stood at the door, half asleep, she heard the sound of a door slam shut to her right, at the far end of the corridor. The one opening onto the small study, as far as she could tell. The corridor light was on. Anxious, she made her way slowly there and put her ear to the door. Sounds of disturbance... there was definitely someone in the room, just as she thought. She knocked on the door... More noises, then the door was opened by a distraught Sir Matthew in pyjamas, who was breathing heavily:

'Ah, it's you, Esther! Something incredible has happened... Look!'

The governess cast an eye around the room, but could see nothing unusual, other than the wardrobe doors, which had been flung wide open.

Behind her, she heard footsteps. Peter and the major had just joined them.

'What's wrong?'

'Can't you see? She's disappeared!' replied Sir Matthew, wide-eyed.

'Who are you talking about?'

'The White Lady! She was in my room... and she left... she came into this room here... *from which she has literally evaporated!*'

4

**The ghost of the fountain**

*September 22*

At the wheel of his service vehicle, Inspector Richard Lewis traversed Buckworth deep in thought. The village, which he knew well, having been born there, still had the same drab appearance—particularly when it was overcast, as it was on that Monday afternoon—with its old brick houses huddled around the church, whose spire rose like the tip of a menacing lance. His background had undoubtedly been the reason he had been assigned to this peculiar case, involving a ghost chase, or more specifically the White Lady chase, which amounted to the same thing in the end. It could only have been due to the influence of Sir Matthew that the powers-that-be had taken the matter seriously, to the point of starting an investigation. The ghost of the White Lady which haunted Buckworth? He'd always heard talk about it, as had everyone in the village. But as far as seeing it?... He'd never heard of any serious testimony on the subject, only gossip and the ravings of drunks or small children. It was true that he'd left Buckworth after grammar school. Twenty years had gone by, during which he felt he'd had quite a successful career. Of athletic build, with a slightly hooked nose and military moustache, he was a naturally imposing figure, especially in view of his new responsibilities.

As he entered the main gate of Buckworth Manor, he could recall only one or two occasions when he had set foot in that holy of holies, probably during village fêtes. The fountain in the middle of the driveway, sporting a graceful nymph, was still there. Like all the village inhabitants, he had envied the occupants of the house, although they were far from being prim and distant. Sir Matthews was a real gentleman, who went regularly to church seriously and had time for everyone. But that didn't make him a saint....

The gravel crunched under the vehicle's tyres as he drew to a halt before the main entrance. What trouble awaited him behind the elegant facade in front of him? Whether trivial or important, it would obviously require delicate handling. In any case, whatever his degree of apprehension, he was a long way from imagining the events that would unfold. Had he known, he would assuredly have turned around immediately.

He gave a deep sigh before getting out of the vehicle.

Moments later, he was ensconced in an armchair in the grand salon, in the company of the whole household. After the introductions and reunions the atmosphere was quite relaxed because, as we have seen, Richard Lewis was a native of those parts.

After writing a few observations in his notebook, he summarised the situation.

'Very well, there have been two strange manifestations of something which we will call, for want of a better name, the White Lady. The first time was roughly three months ago, and the night before last there was another incident, far more disturbing, of which you were the victim, Sir Matthew.'

The lord of the manor grimaced.

'Victim is perhaps a trifle excessive.'

'We'll get back to that. First, we need to establish the facts in chronological order. I believe it was you, Mr. Corsham, who observed the first incident, one night in mid-June.'

'Yes,' replied Peter, who had just lit a cigarette, 'but I can't remember which day exactly.'

'I think it was a Sunday evening,' said Ann tensely. 'I seem to remember we attended church that morning.'

'Possibly,' said Peter, continuing. 'Be that as it may, I'd had trouble sleeping and had gone outside for a smoke. It must have been around midnight. I was near the fountain when—.'

'Was the entrance light on?' asked the inspector.

'No, I don't believe so. But there was enough moonlight to see by. Coming from the main gate, this person came slowly towards me... I straight away thought there was something bizarre about them. Maybe because they moved so silently. I wouldn't swear to it, but it seemed there were no footsteps on the gravel. It was a young woman, all in white... it was so strange that I stood rooted to the spot. It was a warm night, but I suddenly felt a chill... I couldn't see her face, but I sensed she was smiling. And she may well have extended her hand towards me.'

'Do you believe so?' asked the inspector.

Peter clenched his fists uneasily.

'Yes... but I was so surprised... To be frank, I was quite anxious, because all the old village gossip was coming back to me.'

'And so you turned back?'

'No, and I didn't fully understand what happened after that... She stopped and looked at a spot behind me, as if she'd seen something. Then she turned on her heels, but instead of going back to the main gate, she went to her right and cut diagonally across the lawn to the high wire fence... It was darker there because of the tall trees, but I could see her white silhouette clearly. And then I had the impression that she went straight through the fence as if it didn't exist. Then she disappeared... I obviously must have been mistaken, but that's the impression I had at the time. I was in a hell of a state, as Ann can tell you, because she arrived just at that moment.'

The inspector turned to the lady in question, who was just as embarrassed as her husband.

'Yes, I had just joined my husband. He was scared stiff, but I didn't know why. I didn't see the woman at that moment, but I had seen her a minute or so earlier, from our bedroom window. From afar, she just appeared as a shadow. Please understand, I had just woken up to discover myself alone in our bed.'

'Did you turn the light on?'

Ann shrugged her shoulders.

'Yes, probably. That's generally what I do when I get up.'

The policeman nodded his head thoughtfully:

'Well, that's probably what our White Lady saw, the light coming on in the window. That's why she doubled back.'

'Possibly. So I went down, left the house, and joined Peter, who was as rigid as the nymph in the fountain... I have to say I was pretty upset at the time, thinking more about the possibility of cheating on his part than a visit by that creature... Particularly since he seemed lost for words about her departure.'

'That's all very well,' retorted Peter, 'but if I'd started talking about the White Lady, you'd have believed me even less, and probably slapped my face.'

'That's quite possible,' said Ann, with a smile.

'And you would have been right,' mocked Vivian, obviously amused. 'Men always deserve to be slapped!'

'We're in agreement for once,' replied Ann. 'Certain women as well, in my opinion.'

Ignoring the tit-for-tat, Peter continued aggressively:

'I may have been mistaken about the wire fence, which she went through without obstacle, and the same for the smile and the extended hand... But not for the impression of cold! There was something icy about her... A strange chill which she exuded the closer she got.'

'Thank you,' said the inspector. 'Let's just say that up until now the facts, while rather vague, are troubling nevertheless. And you, Sir Matthew, did you also get a cold feeling when the White Lady appeared to you?'

'Yes,' replied the lord of the manor pensively. 'Undoubtedly. But let's begin at the beginning. I had gone to bed early that evening, as I was feeling under the weather. At such times, Vivian and I sleep in separate rooms. I read a bit before going to sleep. And I remember waking up suddenly with my hands and feet very cold. That's not normal, I might add. I lit the bedside lamp, and there she was in front of me, in the middle of the room. Dressed all in white, with a shawl over her head and a long robe or cape. She looked at me out of the darkness. And she smiled.'

'Would you recognise her?'

'Perhaps. I've never seen such a beautiful face.'

'Thanks a lot, darling,' said Vivian, with a pout.

'What happened then?' asked the policeman hurriedly.

'She continued to look at me and I felt increasingly cold as she approached. She looked me up and down, then raised her hand, which she contemplated for a moment before shaking her head... Then, as if changing her mind, she went slowly over to the door, which she opened... As she left, she gave me a smile, as if inviting me to join her... At least, that was the impression I had. I got up and followed her as if I were hypnotised. I saw her at the end of the corridor, going into the small study.'

'Did you see her open and shut the door behind her?'

'Yes, and I felt certain she couldn't escape. Because that young woman, ravishing as she was, still owed me an explanation. I went into the study and shut the door behind me. She must have been hiding, because I couldn't see her. I immediately noticed that the window was closed. I opened the wardrobe doors wide. Nobody inside, nor behind the revolving mirror. As I started to search the rest of the room, there was a knock on the door. It was Esther. Then the others arrived in a bunch, and we determined together that the strange apparition had mysteriously vanished... It would be best, inspector, if you inspected the premises to get a precise idea of the situation.'

'I'll be happy to do that. But for now, we can take note that the two incidents present obvious similarities. The same appearance and comportment of the intruder, the same sensation of cold, and the same mysterious disappearance. Everything suggests we're dealing with the White Lady of local fame.'

'So you believe in that legend, inspector?' asked the major, with the hint of a sneer.

'Not at all. I'm simply summarising the situation. Apart from those two incidents, has she ever appeared in the manor in the past?'

'Not to my knowledge,' replied Sir Matthew. 'But if you ask around in the village, you might find other witnesses.'

'That may be true,' sighed the policeman. 'But it would largely be unsubstantiated. In any case, the main difficulty is that the mysterious visitor hasn't really committed any crime, except possibly trespass. That's why I'm asking you, Sir Matthew, to think carefully about her attitude. Was it truly menacing? From your description, she seems more like a guardian angel.'

'That's a good question,' replied his host, nodding his head. 'It's true that at no time did she make a hostile gesture. But how to tell? There are all kinds of angels, good and bad... A smile isn't always joyful, it can be menacing.'

'And is that what you felt?'

'I don't know. It's hard to say. I think the first time I saw her, after I turned the light on, I had a hell of a shock. Before I got a good look at her, I would have said the worst kind of angel.'

'An angel of death?'

'Precisely, inspector. But afterwards, with her charming smile....'

'You do understand that one can't really call it menace under such circumstances. Not in your case, nor Mr. Corsham's.'

'So what exactly do you plan to do?'

'In the first place, with your permission, I'd like to take a look at the premises.'

A few moments later, Inspector Lewis was examining Sir Matthew's bedroom. The floor was covered by a wall-to-wall carpet, which he inspected thoroughly, discovering nothing suspicious. The same was true for the wardrobe and the cupboards opposite the bed. As for the window, there was no sign of forced entry. He picked up the book lying on the bedside table, next to the lamp.

'Sterne's *A Sentimental Journey*,' he observed with amusement. 'A great classic.'

'Vivian loves it.'

'Is that what you were reading the other night?'

'Um, no... I can't remember where I left the other. Is it important?'

'Not really. What's far more important is how our visitor managed to get in here. I suppose the manor is locked up at night?'

'Yes, and we found no trace of break-in. That said, it isn't a fortress either. The main problem, as I see it, is her disappearance from the other room.'

'We're going there now.'

The small study was at the western extremity of a long corridor leading to ten rooms, situated here and there, of which most were bedrooms. In the middle was the landing of the main staircase, to the right of which, coming up, was Esther's bedroom. Directly opposite was Vivian's bedroom, which adjoined her husband's.

As its name implied, the small study was not a large room. It was in fact rather intimate, with numerous shelves and a table in the centre with a terrestrial globe perched on it. Opposite him, in the west wall, was the only window, framed by heavy curtains. To the right of it, in the far corner, stood a large revolving mirror on a finely chiselled bronze stand. To his left, against the south wall, stood an enormous wardrobe which also served as a walk-in cupboard. Two stools, an armchair, a small circular table and a console made up the rest of the furniture. Richard Lewis examined everything carefully, but found nothing. Turning to his host, he enquired:

'Was the window shut when you came in?'

'Yes. Everyone can confirm that, including Esther.'

'Yes,' affirmed the governess. 'That was the first thing I looked at when Sir Matthew explained the situation to me.'

'What if the intruder had hidden behind the door as you came in, and slipped out afterwards whilst your back was turned?'

'Impossible,' replied Esther. 'I was in the corridor when Sir Matthew entered the room. And the others arrived immediately after me. Nobody could have left through the door at that moment.'

'I can confirm that,' said John Peel. 'I came out into the corridor just as Sir Matthew came in here. And Peter came out just after me.'

The latter nodded his agreement.

'Very well,' the inspector conceded, 'it was impossible. Our intruder could not have escaped from here, according to all your testimonies. Under such circumstances, and without wishing to upset you, Sir Matthew, I fear I must reconsider yours.'

'What?' said their host, clearly offended. 'Do you doubt my word?'

'Of course not. No one is doubting your sincerity. I'm simply asking whether you could have been the victim of a nightmare. In other words, sincerely believing what one feels at the time.'

'I know what a nightmare is, inspector! And like you, I've thought about it—all the time, in fact. But it all happened in one continuous sequence... the young woman left my bedroom, I followed her without taking my eyes off her, I entered after her, and Esther saw me going in. You can treat the two of us as mad, but then you also have to include my son-in-law, who saw her go effortlessly through a wire fence!'

'It was only a hypothesis, sir,' apologised the policeman, blushing. 'A simple hypothesis, like any other, which needs to be explored....'

'I doubt that the solution will be found here,' interjected Ann solemnly.

'What do you mean?'

'That there's someone in the village who, in many people's eyes, could be the infamous White Lady.'

'And who might that be?' asked Sir Matthew in astonishment, taking the words out of the inspector's mouth.

'You know very well,' replied Ann defiantly. 'Young Miss Seagrave. And let me remind you that her mother, the washerwoman, had the same reputation whilst she was still alive.'

'Lethia? The White Lady? Don't you think I'd have recognised her?'

'I don't doubt that for a moment, father dear. In any case, I've lost count of the number of people who've seen her wandering about at night near the pond or the ruins, or elsewhere.'

'Ann, my dear, you're completely mistaken. Those are just old wives' tales.'

'Have you seen her lately?' retorted Ann defiantly.

'Lately? Well....'

'And just who is this Miss Seagrave?' asked Vivian curtly, shooting a furious look at her husband.

'I already told you about her. She's the young woman who reads the cards. She's really gifted, by the way. It was she who foretold a great happiness in my life, just a few days before I met you, darling!'

# 5

## Lethia's Oracle

*September 27*

Who was Lethia Seagrave really? Like many others, Peter Corsham asked himself that question as he was about to visit her that afternoon—one week after the incident in the manor—having decided to find out for himself under the pretext of a consultation. He already knew her slightly, having spoken to her on occasion, which helped. Ann, fully aware of his tactic, was fully supportive, for she suspected the clairvoyant of bewitching her father. 'Discover her ruses and stratagems, the better to counter them,' she had advised him, with cold determination.

Lethia's cottage lay at the end of a road which ran up the side of a small hill to the north of the village. A flight of steps led to a wooden portico which had seen better days and was now partly covered with ivy. A spacious terrace enclosed in glass ran the length of the west side of the building. A crow, cawing from an open panel, did not stop at Peter's approach. Wild creatures were the young woman's only friends and, according to rumour, she had an uncanny knack for healing them.

He pressed the doorbell and the door opened immediately.

'Ah, there you are. I was expecting you.'

'Expecting me?' he gasped. 'Did someone notify you?'

'No. I just knew.'

Peter suppressed a smile. "Prophecies" after the event must be part of the bag of tricks she used to fool the dupes. Having her place him in that category would make his task easier....

Moments later he was ensconced in a leather armchair with lacerated sides, probably due to the cats now sleeping next to their mistress. Lethia herself was seated in a wicker chair surrounded by green plants. She had to be the same age as Ann, but appeared younger because of her wild appearance and unconventional clothes. She was wearing a tight-fitting pair of black silk trousers and an embroidered vermillion jacket of the same material. Slender and supple, she had a narrow face framed with chestnut hair, and large brown eyes with an enigmatic look. She had an undeniably feline look—probably cultivated, thought Peter, careful not to let himself be impressed by the facade. But he had to conceal his hand and appear humble, to be consistent with his request.

'I'm here for a consultation,' he began. 'But I assume you knew that already.'

With a condescending smile, she replied:

'That's usually the reason people come.'

'In fact, it's not really my own future that interests me, although anything on that subject would be welcome. It's about the White Lady, who seems to have set her sights on our family. I suppose you've heard about her most recent appearance?'

'Of course. That's all they talk about in the village. And I even received a visit from a policeman the other day, and not for a consultation. Inspector Lewis, an old acquaintance, in fact,' she added in amusement. 'He seemed to be embarrassed to be questioning me... But that's beside the point. They say, Mr. Corsham, that you yourself were a witness to the incident, and to an earlier one.'

'That's true, but—.'

'Then please begin by telling me about it. There's nothing better than a first-hand account to put things into perspective.'

Although fully aware that the roles were being reversed—it was she, not he, who was asking the questions—Peter carefully recounted the facts, all the while observing her furtively, particularly her big brown eyes, which seemed to be the window into her soul.

'You understand,' he concluded, 'that it's important for us to understand this enigmatic figure better. I'm talking to you just as much as child of the countryside as clairvoyant. You've always lived here. The character of the White Lady must be known to you.'

'I'm not, strictly speaking, a clairvoyant, but I can talk to you about her.'

She had a distant look in her eye as she touched the tips of her fingers together.

'No one can deny her aura, or her influence on the village. I see her as an ethereal figure, swathed in beauty and mystery. It would be futile to try to expose her, to see through her, by gathering the differing accounts of those who claim to have seen her. In the eyes of non-believers, her motives seem as dark as night itself. But to those who understand her, she is an indispensable element of harmony, of the life that the Creator intended us to lead. She is, at the same time, the light and the darkness, as unchangeable and implacable as Time itself.'

She continued in the same vein until Peter interrupted her:

'You speak as if you're one of her most fervent admirers!'

'I am indeed. She has even inspired me to write several poems.'

'So you write poems?'

'From time to time,' replied Lethia, with a slight shrug of her shoulders. 'Sometimes of my own accord, sometimes under inspiration.'

'I'm afraid I don't quite follow.'

'Sometimes I practice what is vulgarly called "automatic writing". Simply put, it's prose written when one is in a trance. Words dictated from a subconscious source. I see that makes you smile.'

'Not at all,' protested Peter. 'Personally, I know nothing about it, I've just heard talk.'

'Perhaps from your father-in-law? I sent him one of my verses recently. Maybe he spoke to you about it?'

After a moment's reflection, Peter shook his head slowly.

'No, doesn't ring a bell. What was it about?'

'I don't remember. I've written so many. The best thing would be to ask him yourself.' She frowned, and added: 'But I wonder if I've properly understood your question about the White Lady, Mr. Corsham. What do you wish to know about her, exactly?'

Peter stroked his moustache before replying, hesitantly:

'Well, what we all need to know is to what degree she represents a threat. And also whether she's likely to reappear in the near future.'

'Now that's much clearer,' she replied, getting up. 'We're going to read the cards. Which do you prefer, the traditional Tarot pack, or oracle cards?'

Peter shrugged his shoulders, thinking to himself that she must take him for a complete idiot.

'You're the one doing the reading, Miss Seagrave. I defer to your experience.'

'Very well. Please wait a moment.'

So saying, she left the room. When she returned a couple of minutes later wearing a violet turban, he had great difficulty suppressing his mirth. Did she think she was more persuasive wearing that cheap junk?

She sat down in her armchair again, drew the table closer and placed a pack of thick cards on it, each decorated with a cabalistic sign on the back.

'Pick three cards and place them face down in front of you.'

After asking him to turn them over slowly in any order, she stared fixedly at them with growing perplexity. After a while, she shook her head.

'Did I do something wrong?' asked Peter.

'Not really. But what I see here is nothing to do with the White Lady. It concerns you. Please concentrate on the first card. It's important, because it concerns your past.'

'I just see a cross, a simple cross.'

'It's the Cross of the Andes, upside down. Have you had dealings with anyone which would have been better avoided?'

'I can't think of any, apart from an insurance broker who caused us a lot of problems.'

'The second card represents the present.'

'It looks like a storm.'

'Yes. It signifies that you're going through a troubling period. But you know that already. You don't need a clairvoyant to tell you that.'

Peter acknowledged the comment and concentrated on the third card, which showed an arrow pointing to the sky.

'That corresponds to my future, I presume.'

'Yes, and it looks fortunate. It looks as though fate will smile on you. But the road will be full of pitfalls and you will need all your resourcefulness to get there. You need to create alliances, or rather one in particular. I can't tell you any more.'

'Hmm,' said Peter, thoughtfully. 'In other words, "Help yourself and heaven will help you"?'

'If you wish.'

'But none of that has anything to do with the White Lady. Will she or will she not pay us another visit?'

'Do you really want to know?' asked Lethia.

'That's what I came for!'

'Well, then, pick another card. You don't need to concentrate this time.'

Hesitatingly, Peter made his choice and turned up a picture of a large feline lurking in a dense forest.

'The jaguar,' said Lethia in a solemn voice, her large brown eyes gleaming disturbingly. 'At least this has the merit of being clear. The jaguar is at the top of the food chain. It fears no predator. It can rain death wherever it wants. In other words, there's nothing good about this card. If the White Lady pays you another visit, and there's every reason to think she will, it won't be harmless. Like the jaguar, she has the power of life or death.'

6

**A passing angel**

*October 4*

The air was stiflingly humid that night. Dense mists from Buckworth pond spread slowly along the dirt path which led through some woods to the village. It was past eleven o'clock. Who would be crazy enough to be wandering around in such circumstances? No one. Nonetheless, Billy, Jack and Harry had arranged to meet. The three ten-year-old boys were not amongst the brightest in the village. Particularly Harry, a veritable tearaway with numerous petty thefts to his credit, detested by adults but adored by his companions. Amongst those upon whom he exercised his influence were Billy, the baker's son, and Jack, whose parents ran the *Three Keys* inn.

Shivering, and staring at the clouds of mist floating above the pond, Billy complained:

'I hope you didn't make us come here for nothing, Harry. I don't like it here.'

'As if this is the first time we've been here, wimp!'

'Yes, but not at night and in such weather.'

'And you, Jack?' sneered Harry, with a defiant grin. 'What about it? Have I ever let you down?'

'No, of course not,' stammered the other. 'But with all the stories going around these days....'

'Are you also chicken? Don't tell me you believe those ghost stories! White Ladies are like Santa Claus, they don't exist. Stop staring at the pond as if an army of spooks is going to come out. Follow me, I've something much more interesting to show you.'

At that, the three companions set off along the path through the woods. Harry, who was carrying a torch, stopped suddenly to shine it behind one of the bushes. To their alarm, his two friends could see a fox caught in the jaws of a trap.

'And there's the loot,' bragged Harry. 'I wasn't the one to set the trap, it was Leonard the poacher. I've been tracking him and I know where he places all his traps.'

'So what?' asked Jack. 'Are you going to turn him in?'

'Of course not, idiot. The idea is to take them before he does.'

'Look,' said Billy, 'it's still alive, by the looks of it, poor thing.'

'I don't think so,' retorted Jack, leaning over to get a better look. 'See, the blood is already dry.'

'I know that,' said Harry. 'It was already dead when I found it this afternoon. Let's go back to the pond and talk about it.'

By the time they got back to the pond, the mist had dispersed slightly and they could see the silver halo of the moon.

'Fox's fur can be worth quite a bit if you know the right people,' explained Harry, 'and I do. The plan is to find out when one of Leonard's traps catches something and beat him to it. If we take it in turns, we can take quite a bit of his loot.'

'That sounds good,' said Jack, 'but aren't we going to be taking a lot of risks for only a small reward?'

'Risks? What risks? Do you think Leonard's going to complain?'

'No, but even so....'

'No risk, no gain. Haven't you heard that?' He flashed his wristwatch and went on: 'Did you think it was my drunken father that gave me this? You're like sheep, you two, like sheep chewing grass.'

'You can go chew grass yourself,' retorted Billy angrily.

In response, Harry tore some leaves from a nearby bush, stuffed them in his mouth, and began to chew them.

In the light of the moon, which had grown in intensity, Billy examined the bush more closely and declared:

'I don't think this is very edible. Someone told me— .'

'Shut up,' mumbled Harry, continuing to chew.

'No, really, you should spit it out.'

'I said shut up.'

But, after a short while, Harry pulled a face.

'Ugh, this stuff is bitter.'

He spat it out and started to explain his money-making project. But after a quarter-of-an-hour, he pulled another face and clutched his stomach. His friends suggested they go back home, but he insisted on developing his plan. Suddenly, as if overcome by fatigue, he sat down on a tree stump.

'Are you all right?' asked Billy anxiously.

'It's nothing. It'll pass.'

'There's someone there,' muttered Jack quietly.

'What are you talking about?'

'Down there, on the path.'

'I can't hear anything,' groaned Harry, his head in his hands.

'Take a look then.'

Following their companion's gaze, Harry and Billy could just make out a pale, indistinct form coming slowly towards them, gradually becoming white and feminine. When it was within ten yards of them, they could see it was a ravishingly beautiful young woman wearing a cape. There was a shawl over her head which shimmered in the silver light of the moon.

'Stay where you are, lads. No blooming girl is going to scare us.'

But, despite his exhortation, his two companions stepped aside whilst the apparition continued straight towards Harry. All three of them could now see her face, white as snow, but smiling. Harry seemed frozen to the spot as the apparition raised her hand towards him. When she touched him on the brow he staggered and dropped to the ground. She turned her head to the left and right, as if to bestow one last smile upon them, then turned on her heel and started back to where she had come from. Terrified, Jack and Billy watched her slowly disappear into the darkness of the woods.

Then they rejoined their companion, inert on the ground.

'He doesn't look well,' muttered Jack.

'Not well at all,' agreed his friend.

'Harry, wake up!' cried Jack, slapping him several times, to no effect.

Then, eyes wide with fear, he turned to Billy.

'What do we do now?'

## 7

## An exceptional adversary

*Achilles Stock's account*

*London, October 9*

Ensconced in an armchair in Owen's comfortable apartment in St. James's Square, I was reading the newspaper whilst observing my friend out of the corner of my eye. His corpulent figure moved back and forth, but his eyes never left the mantelpiece, on which was standing a magnificent piece of Chinese porcelain. It was difficult to gauge his mood, which seemed to be in the grip of conflicting sentiments. Normally he was more incisive. I had come to London to spend a few days in his company, having not seen him for quite some time. He had changed, no doubt due to the article in *The Times*, which had lauded his talents as a detective, after he had succeeded in dismantling an important antique-smuggling ring masterminded by an American dealer.

'Is it seeing your face on the front page of the newspaper that has affected you?' I asked, hazarding a guess.

'Amongst other things.'

'The threats to your person made by your enemy upon his arrest, no doubt?'

'I have nothing to do with that overdressed Yankee, Achilles. He was an easy adversary, completely devoid of any artistic sensitivity, despite his profession. Which is why he lost. My principal enemy is something else.'

'And what would that be?'

'My ego. I've been fighting it desperately over the years, as you know, but that excessively laudatory article has revived it in a big way... But enough of me, my good friend. Tell me instead what you think of my new acquisition.'

So saying, he lifted the vase off the mantelpiece and handed it to me to examine.

'A Chinese porcelain of exquisite manufacture,' I replied after a while.

'But which period? Ming or Qing?'

'I would say between the two.'

'I see,' he mocked. 'You sensed a trap and opted for prudence. 'That's not worthy of your standing as head of a porcelain manufacturer in the Cotswolds.'

'Maybe,' I admitted irritably. 'I know you only too well, Owen.'

'Be that as it may, you've got it all wrong. The vase is only an imitation, which I would not qualify as vulgar, because I, renowned art critic that I am, was also fooled.'

Fists clenched, he continued:

'I've had it appraised, and there's no doubt.'

'Where did it come from?'

'I bought it from a pawnbroker in Whitechapel. It's not the first time I've had dealings with him.'

'What do you plan to do?'

My friend had adopted a position in front of the hearth, and the light from the flames sculpted a sardonic expression on his face. He replied:

'Take revenge.'

'How, for goodness sake?'

'The punishment shall fit the crime. We're going to pay him a little visit tonight.'

'Don't think for a moment that I'm going to accompany you on a punitive expedition. You've lost your mind, my friend. Don't count on me!'

Owen shook his head without losing his vindictive expression.

'I can assure you we're not going to go there armed with cudgels. Just a brief visit to the shop, to hit him where it hurts most. We'll simply take a few of his best pieces and throw them in the Thames. That way there'll be no personal profit for us, just a lesson in good manners.'

As I was still catching my breath, he threw his head back and roared with laughter.

'My dear Achilles, if you could only see your face,' he cackled. 'How could you possibly think I would do such a thing? I was only testing you.'

'Testing me how?'

'To see how far you would follow me.'

'To Hell, perhaps.'

'In a way,' he replied, his tone suddenly changed. 'Because the case I've been asked to investigate, and for which I shall need your help, concerns a diabolical creature. An exceptional adversary, such as we have never faced.'

'Are you sure? What about the Wolf of Fenrir, or the Lord of Misrule? Phantoms, invisible murderers, werewolves....'

'Worse than that, Achilles. Here it concerns the supreme enemy.'

'You intrigue me, Owen,' I said cheerfully, having forgiven the dubious farce. 'Let's see... Hades, Prince of the Underworld?'

'You're cold.'

'Well then, perhaps Satan himself.'

'You're getting warmer, but that's still not it.'

'Well then, what?' I asked irritably.

'The most implacable enemy of all, against whom one can do nothing. In other words: *Death itself*.'

I sat speechless, as he stood immobile in front of the hearth.

'Let me explain,' he continued, 'or you're going to burst a vein. You've heard of the White Ladies, I presume? The White Ladies the country-folk talk about in their thatched cottages, who appear at nightfall. Sometimes they're just harmless ghosts, bewailing the injustices they suffered during their lifetimes. At other times, they can be vengeful spirits, the sort we associate with the angel of death, the hand of destiny which seeks out its victims... The one seen in Buckworth, in Oxfordshire, seemed initially to be in the first category. As she beat a retreat, she went through a wire fence just like a ghost. That happened at the residence of one Sir Matthew Richards at the beginning of the summer. And she did it again a few weeks ago in the same place, this time entering the owner's bedroom before taking refuge in a room from which she mysteriously vanished. Up to that point, she had not harmed anyone. But then she reappeared a few days later, not as an inoffensive angel, but as an evil one!

'It was almost midnight, and three young boys were playing near the village pond. One of them, named Harry, chewed on several twigs of hemlock, either by accident or out of bravado. He spat some of it out and started to feel ill. That's when our White Lady appeared... Just like death coming to find him, she placed her glacial hand on him and he dropped stone dead to the ground in front of his terrified friends. The autopsy attributed his death to hemlock poisoning.

'Ordinarily, one would not have given any credence to the fantastic testimonies of the other two boys, but the previous incidents gave pause for thought and even gave the inspector in charge of the investigation grey hairs. One Lewis, without much experience, as far as I can gather, who ended up contacting Scotland Yard. There, our old friend Superintendent Wedekind, busy, according to him, with too many other cases—and only too happy to drop this brain-teaser in my lap—asked me to give young Lewis a hand. I neglected to mention that, as if all the foregoing were not enough, a local clairvoyant accurately predicted the drama... That's a brief summary of what awaits us, my dear Achilles. I hope I can count on you. We'll take the first train from Paddington tomorrow morning.'

'To face Death or go to Hell!' I exclaimed. 'What a charming prospect. I would have preferred a deserted Pacific island populated with exquisite creatures.'

'From that point of view, my dear friend, permit me to remind you that it's in Hell that the most beautiful creatures are to be found. And there will be no lack of them in our investigation: the fortune-teller, Sir Matthew's young wife and his two daughters. All young and pretty, according to Lewis, and potentially the only suspects, because of their physical appearance, to be hiding behind the mask of our mysterious White Lady. In other words, our mission will be to concentrate almost exclusively on the fair sex. Are you game?'

'So be it,' I replied, with a feigned commiseration. 'Leaving you to face that terrifying imbroglio alone is more than my conscience can bear.'

## 8

### Hemlock, the White Lady and the fox

*Achilles Stock's account (continued)*

*October 10*

In the late morning, Owen, Inspector Lewis and myself were on the banks of the pond, near the spot where young Harry had met his fate. Under the overcast sky, it was a colourless tableau, but for the blue-green plumage of a duck paddling on the murky waters.

'We interviewed the two other boys separately,' explained the inspector in his grating voice. 'There were no discrepancies at all in their accounts. We found the fox in the trap exactly where they had described.' He pointed to a tree stump to our right. 'That's what Harry sat on, and over there are the hemlock bushes, one of which has freshly broken branches. We even found the sprigs he spat out and others in his stomach, proving it was a case of poisoning. And that's all. No suspicious marks on the body.'

'And nobody had thought to clear the bushes beforehand?' I asked.

The policeman shrugged:

'As you can see, it's a wild area, usually only frequented by amateur fishermen. And most people around here know their poisonous plants, including the kids like Billy, who tried to warn the victim. It was around eleven o'clock when they arrived here, and around half-past when Harry swallowed the deadly poison. Twenty minutes after that, he died, following the arrival of the White Lady. By midnight, Jack and Billy were back in the village at the *Three Keys* inn—where you have rooms reserved—which had just closed its doors. The landlords are Jack's parents. Even though they didn't believe their son and his friend at first, they eventually agreed to follow them here and arrived here at quarter-past twelve.

'And there we are,' continued the inspector with a sigh. 'It's basically a banal and tragic accident, with kids issuing stupid challenges, as is often the case. An accident in clearly established circumstances, if you exclude the strange apparition.'

Whilst Owen stood silently observing the frolics of the duck, I asked:

'As I understand it, little Harry was the village pest, thoroughly detested by everyone.'

'Quite so. But to go from there to eliminating him... As I told you, it was a purely accidental death. Murder is completely ruled out.'

'That leaves the enigma of the White Lady, who just happened to arrive at the appointed time, like Death claiming its victim!'

Lewis looked solemnly at his companions, then gave a deep sigh:

'When I was asked to investigate the incident at the manor, I had a sudden apprehension... I sensed instinctively that there would be complications... but not to that point, believe me. At first I doubted the testimony of old Sir Matthew and his entourage about creatures appearing and disappearing, as if by magic. I thought it must be some sort of collective hallucination, triggered by rumours and legend. I thought the same thing when I questioned Jack and Billy. But their story never varied an inch. They affirmed having seen the White Lady coming along the path towards their sick friend and extending her hand to him just before he dropped dead. Afterwards, she retraced her steps at the same slow pace. They were terrified, which is completely understandable... And why would anyone think for a moment that they had invented the story? To lessen their role because they felt more or less responsible? That wouldn't have changed anything, by the way. Unless they were the most incorrigible liars in the county, I can guarantee they told the truth—or what they believed to be the truth.'

'Did they mention a sudden sensation of cold as the stranger approached?'

'More or less. But in view of the fact they were terrified and the temperature was dropping....'

'Were they able to give you a detailed description of the apparition?' asked Owen.

'Yes. She was wearing a white cape, with a shawl of the same colour on her head, quite loose-fitting, which she wore like a shroud. So much so that they couldn't see her hair.'

'What about her face?'

'That of a pretty young woman, smiling, with a complexion as white as snow. But one they couldn't identify... Just as in the case of Sir Matthew and his nephew, incidentally.'

'Couldn't one get the same result with artful make-up and white cream?' I asked. 'Or simply with a mask?'

'Maybe. But according to them, it was indubitably the figure and manner of walking of a woman. But, Hell's Bells, what's all this farce about? And how could anybody, anybody at all, have foreseen the accident in order to play the ghost at the precisely right time? It doesn't make any sense!'

'Yet someone seems to have forecast it, more or less, isn't that so?' asked Owen, with the shadow of a smile. 'Lethia Seagrave, our local clairvoyant.'

'Yes, but she only talked of a future intervention of the White Lady after Peter Corsham had asked her about it. It would be best if you questioned them both on the subject. That said, everyone in the manor had been notified by Corsham, and I expect it didn't take long for the whole village to know. Which means that everyone knew about a probable new manifestation, and any one of them could have dressed up as the White Lady, leaving aside the motive and the extraordinary timing for the moment.

'As for Lethia, I've known her since she was a little girl. She's an enigma in her own right, and in many ways. She seems to have certain special gifts, from which she makes a living. She has a small salon in London, which she visits regularly. I'm waiting for additional information about that, and about her finances generally.'

'In short,' I observed, 'she seems to be your principal suspect?'

'Yes, but suspect of what?' retorted the policeman in exasperation. 'Of playing at ghosts, of fortune-telling, or of provoking an accident somehow? In order to increase her notoriety?'

'Had she an alibi for the time of the incident?'

'No. She was asleep in her bed, like almost everyone else at that hour. Almost... And that's another mystery,' added Lewis, mopping his brow with his sleeve. 'If we start with the assumption that our unknown stranger is a pretty woman, there's another one in this business who hasn't been very clear in her explanations... I'm talking about Vivian, the young wife of Sir Matthew. Vivian Marsh is her maiden name. Even though she didn't offer up the information herself, she was in the *Three Keys* up until closing time, just before the boys saw the White Lady appear. Alone, sitting discreetly in a corner of the saloon bar. She had arrived half-an-hour earlier. The landlord and several customers had recognised her, and she didn't deny it subsequently. Incidentally, she often frequents the inn, though seldom alone. She had slept in her own bedroom in the manor that night, so no one had noticed her leave. But even stranger is her explanation....

'According to her, she had a rendezvous with an old friend—a certain Andrew Moog—who had sent her a message during the day asking her for an urgent meeting to discuss an unspecified problem. Privately, she had confessed that he was an old flame, a sleazy individual she did not wish her husband to find out about. Which would explain her silence, expecting nothing good to come out of the meeting. But in the end, the aforementioned Moog didn't turn up. I'm trying to find out more about him, but there's nothing for the moment.'

'Curious indeed,' I said thoughtfully. 'Purely from the chronology of events, she could have played the White Lady in front of the kids.'

'Have you seen the message?' asked Owen.

Inspector Lewis shook his head.

'No. She threw it straight in the fire. At least, that's what she said. But with her, you understand, I couldn't insist as I did with the children. The whole business is very delicate. Truly astounding, in fact, like a fairy tale, but officially we haven't an offence. Regarding little Harry, it was clearly an accidental death, and the apparition of the White Lady can be put down to hallucinations on the part of the boys. There's no other way.'

After yet another sigh, the policeman turned to my friend.

'So, what do you think, Mr. Burns? I know you're held in high regard by the powers that be, and I don't doubt your competence, but you must admit it's a very puzzling business.'

'To be frank, it's what I expected,' replied Owen, his hands behind his back, facing the pond. 'And I fear other surprises await us. But, to answer your question, what escapes me totally for the moment is the motive behind all these doings, assuming there is one. A bad joke, an omen, a symbolic act, or a divine one? We have no idea. Perhaps it will become clearer after hearing from the occupants of Buckworth

Manor.'

'You'll be seeing them this afternoon. I've informed them of your visit.'

'In fact, Inspector Lewis, I believe you are the best placed to address the problem.'

His remark surprised me, to say the least. It was not my friend's habit to turn to others to find the truth.

'You have the advantage of us,' he continued, 'because you know the area. You were born in the village, I believe?'

The policeman, visibly surprised by the confidence placed in him, stroked his moustache with a smile.

'Well, yes. I spent my first fifteen years here.'

'I imagine life must have been much harder then?'

'Of course. Particularly since I hadn't been lucky enough to have been born in a manor. My mother, bless her soul, lived from hand to mouth her whole life to put me through school and to keep me on the straight and narrow. I lost my father when I was very young and have no memories of him. But we were happy. We had the open air, the forest and our liberty. Little Lethia must have been six or seven years old when I left, and our paths never crossed after that. It was a funny feeling seeing her again, and I must admit it was embarrassing to have to question her the other day, as if she was a suspect. I think she also must have had a difficult childhood. And she never had a father at all, or at least not a known one, if you see what I mean. But, despite everything, she survived. She's quite well educated, despite her wild airs, and I have to admit she's grown into a very pretty girl.'

'Or a pretty ghost?' said Owen jocularly.

'I understand your question, Mr. Burns. It's difficult to say. It's true she's rather special. But what I fear, after what I've seen these last few days, is her getting the blame for all this. She's thought of as some kind of magician. Some even think she might be our famous White Lady. And I'm not just talking about recent incidents. There are those who claim to have seen her wandering the alleyways in her night shirt, with a haggard expression on her face.'

'Wait a minute,' I interjected. 'The White Lady existed long before she was born, didn't she?'

'I know. But I'm afraid logic and gossip rarely go together. Particularly since Lethia is the daughter of Mary Seagrave, the washerwoman with a bad reputation that the birth of a child out of wedlock did nothing to improve. I didn't know her, but she was apparently very pretty with long black curly locks.'

'Like mother, like daughter, in fact,' observed Owen. 'Thus does the flame of the White Lady pass from generation to generation. There's a certain logic to it, admit it. But tell me, Inspector, from your own memories, what kinds of creature were those White Ladies? Pale ghosts, vengeful spirits? Or the hand of fate, like the one who called young Harry back to her?'

Lewis scratched his head, as if to jog his memory.

'I don't remember any case like that of the unfortunate lad. Nor any other involving sudden death. That said, her presence was often interpreted as an evil omen.'

'Very well,' said Owen, consulting his watch. 'Now let's get something to eat. It's nearly midday and the country air has given me an appetite!'

## 9

### The man with two faces

*Achilles Stock's account (continued)*

'... Every cloud has a silver lining,' declared Sir Matthew from the depths of his armchair. 'That incident, tragic though it may be, at least has the merit of confirming my own misadventure. For I know Lewis—whom I saw delivered as a baby—to be a level-headed sort... I hope you'll take me seriously from now on.'

It was slightly after two. Owen and I were at the manor, having been introduced by the inspector. He had accompanied us upstairs in order to show us Sir Matthew's bedroom and the small study, where Owen had spent a long time examining the revolving mirror. After that, Lewis excused himself on the grounds of not wanting to influence our investigation.

With his grey hair carefully smoothed back, enhanced by his wine-coloured jacket and his upright posture, the lord of the manor cut a fine figure. The somewhat severe expression on his angular face was tempered by his warm smile. He seemed very alert for his age, but his greyish cheek bones and slightly purplish nostrils were possible signs of ill health.

'And you, Mr. Burns, what do you think? I know your reputation, of course, and I've read the newspaper accounts of your latest exploit. You're to be congratulated for putting that scoundrel away.'

'He gave himself away. I merely encouraged him,' said my friend, with unbecoming modesty.

'Well played anyway. I hope you'll be just as brilliant in our present case. What are your first impressions? Do you doubt our account, like so many others?'

'I would not be here if that were the case,' replied Owen, with a tranquil assurance. 'I tell myself that the facts are so extraordinary they could not have been invented. And, as you yourself observed, the circumstances of young Harry's death confirm that we must take the matter very seriously.'

'I'm glad to hear it, sir. It's always a pleasure to deal with true professionals. It's been my guiding principle my entire life. That saying, have you any more questions?'

'A few. Do you have any idea how the White Lady managed to get into your bedroom?'

'By the door, I assume. I'm a heavy sleeper. What concerns me more is her incredible escape from the small study.'

'That's a mere detail for now,' replied Owen disdainfully. 'I do have a few ideas, but we'll leave the subject for the time being, until I have more information. What I'd also like to know is your impression when you saw her appear.'

Sir Matthew stroked his chin and replied:

'A shock, whose importance I didn't appreciate until later. And in retrospect, given what happened at the pond, I'm still shaken. I believe I understand more now. When I think about it, there was nothing friendly about her smile, and the outcome might have been considerably worse if Esther hadn't arrived so quickly.'

'That's possible,' agreed Owen. 'And when the White Lady approached your son-in-law in the park in early summer, she seemed to have been perturbed in the same fashion by the unexpected arrival of his wife.'

'That's right. I hadn't made the connection,' agreed the old man.

'One last question, if I may, on the subject of Lethia Seagrave, whom you know very well, according to rumour.'

The lord of the manor's expression changed.

'Yes, I know her, quite well in fact, as I regularly make use of her services. Whatever they say about her, she's very gifted and very instinctive. Her visions are extraordinary and have seldom disappointed me.'

'Opinions in the village seem divided.'

'That's jealousy, rancour and ingratitude. She's provided many services and cured many people. Have they forgotten?'

'According to Inspector Lewis, she also has a small office in London.'

'Yes, she does, and I've sent her a number of clients there, who have never complained about her services, by the way.'

'Well then,' replied Owen mischievously, 'I'll probably be the next.'

'I'm sure a man of your qualities will appreciate her services. That said, I understand the sense of your question, Mr. Burns. It won't be long before rumour has it that she was responsible for that boy's tragic death. I'll tell you frankly—and I have a long experience of human nature—nothing could be further from the truth. And I have confidence in your intelligence: you'll feel the same way once you've met her.'

Owen nodded politely and remarked:

'I hope all these events haven't disturbed the family atmosphere.'

'I don't think so,' replied Sir Matthew. 'As you know, my elder daughter has come to stay with us, together with her husband, who was taken for dead only a few months ago. That news, and my recent marriage, have been like a breath of fresh air in the household. That rascal John, I unjustly underrated him. You need to know....' Whereupon he rambled on about his voyage to India, of no interest here. Our next witness was the aforementioned major himself.

'I had never heard of the White Lady before coming here,' declared John Peel, 'but it's as if she was an old friend by my side during five long and horrible years. If I'd had the power, I'd have called her many times to end my suffering. Don't think I'm angling for sympathy, gentlemen. I'm simply trying to describe my mental state at the time. Death would have been a deliverance. But I don't regret fighting, because I was lucky enough to find Margot again and enjoy a comfortable existence here.'

The major was a man of robust constitution in his late thirties, even though his prematurely grey hair made him appear older. He had clearly not fully recovered his forces—the cheeks of his furrowed face still remained hollow—but one sensed by his confident smile that he was well on his way. He inspired sympathy, although there was something bestial about the left side of his face, streaked with ugly scars, particularly when seen from profile.

'So you see,' he continued, 'this story about the White Lady doesn't bother me unduly. Having returned from Hell, one no longer fears death.'

'And you never visited Buckworth in the past?' asked Owen.

'No. I'm only now discovering the village, with its fair share of gossips, just like any other. And, to anticipate one of your questions, I know nothing about any of the rumours.'

'Nevertheless,' asked Owen. 'What is your feeling, as a man of action, about the situation? I'm referring to the White Lady, of course.'

Major Peel made an evasive gesture.

'It's difficult to say. For me, it's a bit like looking in the mirror. There are two views. One is clean and rational, the point of view of a soldier, rejecting all the nonsense out of hand. The other is mysterious and disturbing, where anything seems possible. I know from experience that one can soon feel out of one's depth in a perilous situation, which was the case that night when we rushed to the small study to help my father-in-law and Esther, both of whom were seized by panic. But that was not my hardest test upon my return to this country.'

'Ah!' exclaimed Owen. 'Is there another mysterious fact to be added to the file?'

'No, I'm simply speaking of my reunion with Margot. I was sure I would never see her again, at least as her husband. The happiness of holding her in my arms after so many years, was more beneficial to me than all the medical procedures.'

'That's understandable.'

'In the space of a few seconds, it was as if all my misfortunes had disappeared at the wave of a magic wand. We decided to bury the past. That must have been harder for her, because I understood that she just got engaged... But one doesn't disappear for five years without consequences.'

'It's incredible all the same,' said Owen, lighting a cigarette. 'I've always said that an eventful life is the only life worth living. But you've had more than your fill. I'm also thinking about what your wife must have felt when she identified what she thought was your body. What an ordeal for her. And yet, in a way, I wonder if her mistake wasn't beneficial.'

'In what way?' asked the major with a frown.

'The anguish of uncertainty is often worse than the reality of death.'

'Yes,' the other replied after a while. 'You're right. I hadn't looked at it that way.'

At which point John Peel left. His wife took his place shortly afterwards. Margot was a pretty woman with a slightly Bohemian air, despite her elegant attire. Her gaze was at once friendly, distant and mysterious. My friend exercised all his talent to question her about the incident which cost young Harry his life. She confirmed what her husband had told us previously: that they had gone to bed early. Their bedroom was adjacent to Sir Matthew's, but they hadn't been disturbed by any peculiar noises.

Owen's intention was clearly to determine whether it would have been possible for her to have slipped out to play the role of the White Lady at the pond. Technically it was possible, but I had difficulty imagining that a woman like her could be so sly and calculating. There was something seraphic about her, and the mystery of the White Lady seemed scarcely to trouble her. Her childhood memories on the subject were vague and close to what we knew already. But a question from Owen about her father's remarriage touched a nerve.

'What was my reaction when I heard the news?' she asked with a puzzled look... 'I don't know how to describe it. In fact, my sister told me in a letter. It was an enormous surprise! I was already in shock after having found my husband again. To cap it all, the way we made the acquaintance of our future mother-in-law on the train to Buckworth....'

Whereupon she described the practical joke Vivian had played on them regarding the accursed suitcase, which Owen found very amusing.

'Finally, what do you think of her in retrospect?'

'We've become more or less friends. And even my sister, who was very much against her at the beginning, has warmed to her a little. That saying, she still views her as a gold-digger. But we're able to play bridge together without enduring a torrent of sarcasm. And it has to be said that the recent events in the village have tempered the atmosphere as well.'

'I see, madam,' said Owen. 'But you haven't really answered my question.'

Her eyes, evasive up until then, suddenly locked on Owen's:

'I'm not normally bellicose, sir. I've known enough misfortune, and I've learnt how to adapt to the strangest situations. I'm not a fool and I don't consider my father one, either. At least, not today. We've buried the hatchet and we're all the better for it.'

Owen, surprised by the trenchant response, fell silent for a moment. When he questioned her about Lethia Seagrave, she was equally unforthcoming. Having lost touch with her for many years, she claimed to be unable to form an opinion. Others in the manor were better qualified.'

After she had left, I asked my friend what he thought of her.

'I don't know,' he grumbled.

'I couldn't help noticing,' I said mockingly, 'that your legendary charm was ineffective this time.'

He shrugged his shoulders.

'One can't please everyone. But I haven't said my final word, and I haven't crossed her off my list of White Lady suspects.'

Esther was next into the room. She was an elderly but distinguished looking woman, dressed all in black. She had a beautiful face with high cheek bones, scarcely affected by the passage of time. There again, Owen hit a brick wall, at least initially. The governess gave clear answers without revealing her feelings. She did concede, however, that her master had changed somewhat since his marriage, that there had been certain reorganisations in the manor as a consequence, that the considerable difference in ages could sometimes create tension, that harmony did not always reign, but that was more an assessment than a judgment. On the subject of Lethia—a stranger to the manor—her reply was less formal.

'I don't think anyone in the village knows her true nature. There are contradicting opinions. Personally, I think the truth is somewhere in the middle. There must be some part that's true... In any case, she's not like the others, for certain.'

'Sir Matthew seems to like her,' said Owen, with feigned detachment.

'That's true. He's always supported her, come hell or high water, as they say. But if he believes in her powers, that's his business, not mine.'

'Speaking of powers, it's said that she predicted the last intervention of the White Lady.'

'That's what Peter told us, after he'd questioned her. He spoke of an unfortunate event, but only vaguely. It would be better if you were to ask him personally.'

'And what do you think of the White Lady? Because you witnessed one of her apparitions in the upstairs corridor, I believe? Could you retrace her exact movements?'

As she was doing so, we noticed a lessening in the clarity of her explanation the longer she talked. Her delivery became disjointed, betraying more and more her emotion.

'In hindsight, it all seems incredible, astonishing... Everything happened very quickly. To be truthful, I was worried about Sir Matthew, whose heart is not very strong. He tried to put a brave face on, but I could sense his profound anxiety. And what happened to young Harry hasn't helped.'

'Ah?' replied Owen in astonishment. 'We've just talked to him, and he didn't appear particularly perturbed.'

Esther leant forward and lowered her voice:

'You have to be a psychologist, Mr. Burns, no offence intended. I've known Sir Matthew for a very long time, perhaps longer than anyone. I think he doesn't want to lose face in front of his young bride, which is normal. But deep down, I'm sure he's eaten up with anxiety. I know what he thinks and what torments him because I feel exactly the same way. We've always worked like that: without exchanging a word, we understand each other. I don't know what's about to happen here, nor even whether it's to do with the White Lady... but, mark my words, nothing good will come out of it.'

## 10

### Vivian's alibi

*Achilles Stock's account (continued)*

After the governess had left, I turned to my friend:
'Speaking of the disappearance from the small study, Owen, when we were interviewing Sir Matthew you said you had three ideas about it. Were you bluffing?'
'No, why?'
'Then explain yourself. I'm all ears.'
'Let me think... Ah, yes. The first was that Sir Matthew was lying for some reason. The second was based on the layout of the premises, but there are still a few technical points I need to know. As for my third idea, it's the most audacious of the three but perhaps the simplest, it's—.'
Just at that moment there was a knock on the door. Vivian Richards appeared, and with her an aura of sensuality permeated the room. She was wearing a bright red satin robe which suited her olive complexion and contrasted well with her long black tresses. A twinkling smile, big dark eyes and perfect legs completed the picture. I told myself that, with all these elements, she moved to the top of the list of White Lady suspects.

Owen tried to put her at ease—as if she needed it—by avoiding a direct question. After a friendly preamble, he said gaily:
'Let me guess. You have French roots, do you not? It's very subtle, but I detect a hint of an accent.'
'Yes and no. I was born in England, but I've lived a long time on the continent and my father was from Martinique. After a stay at the Sorbonne, I went to Africa to follow a young soldier who... But if I tell you the story of my life, gentlemen, we'll be here for a long time.'
'Oh, I love stories, including those about mysterious suitcases.'
'I see. Will I never live that down?'
'Speaking personally, I'm not reproaching you about anything. I

like nothing more than a good joke and a surprise. It would be a dull life without them. However....' He paused to leaf through his notebook. 'Ah, here we are, Andrew Moog. That's the name of the old friend whom you were to meet last Saturday in the *Three Keys*, isn't it?'

'Yes,' she sighed. 'Inspector Lewis already questioned me on the matter.'

'And there's no trace of him for the moment.'

'That's not surprising. Andrew's always been restless. It's perhaps for that reason that... But is it really important?'

Ignoring the question, Owen asked:

'So he was an old flame?'

'Yes, but not one who left a favourable impression. My husband knows he hasn't been the only man in my life, but I prefer to spare him certain details, all the same.'

'When was the last time you saw Moog?'

'About two years ago, in Belgium.'

'So why this rendezvous two years later?'

'I've no idea. But since he was perpetually broke, I assume he intended to ask me for money, having no doubt learnt of my recent marriage.'

'Did you bring any money with you?'

'Certainly not! And even if he'd hoped to get paid for some passionate love letter, I wouldn't have given him a penny.'

'Do you think he'll turn up again?'

'I certainly hope not!'

'If that happens, you would do well to alert Inspector Lewis or me. But I want to go back to that night. The inn closed its doors at around twenty-to-twelve. What did you do after that?'

'Afterwards? I came directly back here... Without playing the role of the White Lady, if that's your question.'

'I would like to believe you, madam, but I need to be clear, because you said nothing about your little sortie earlier.'

'For the obvious reason, which I explained. Do I have to say it again?'

'No. On the other hand, we'd like to hear your view of recent events.'

'In other words, who's hiding behind the enigmatic and sublime

White Lady?' she asked, with a note of irony. 'Maybe me?' she added, stretching out her leg, letting us guess at its perfect curve.

'You certainly have the right physique,' admitted Owen, a note of admiration in his voice. 'Everything leads us to believe she's very pretty... According to several testimonies, including that of your husband.'

'But don't you think he'd have recognised me the other night in his bedroom?'

'The problem is that he couldn't recognise anyone.'

'Then why not look elsewhere, outside the house? And, who knows, maybe the intruder was simply wearing a mask.'

'Do you suspect anyone?'

'Yes and no. I'm not one to join in any chorus, but on the other hand there's no smoke without fire.'

'Are you alluding to the village soothsayer?'

Vivian shrugged her shoulders.

'She predicted the events at the pond, didn't she, more or less. Not to mention her dubious morality. If I hadn't been there, if I hadn't met Matthew, who's to say she wouldn't now be occupying my place?'

Owen suppressed a smile.

'It's true we've already had other testimonies hinting at the same thing. How is everyone coping here, by the way? Is there a pleasant atmosphere?'

The young woman let out a deep sigh.

'I'm making a great effort to see that there is. Harmony sometimes comes at a great price, Mr. Burns, believe me.'

After a word of agreement, my friend thanked her and watched her admiringly until she shut the door behind her. Then he confided:

'Did you see those ankles, Achilles? Absolutely perfect!'

'Oh, I hadn't noticed.'

'Then I don't know what you were goggling at. But let's move on. Let us see how Mrs. Ann Corsham's fare in comparison.'

The younger daughter of Sir Matthew was also a fine filly, but of a more Nordic type than Vivian and more distant, less accessible. With her golden hair tied in a chignon, her haughty air, her pale blue eyes and her delicate features, she resembled the Snow Queen. In other words, a perfect White Lady, who in my opinion displaced Vivian at the top of the list of suspects. A brief glance at Owen confirmed that he shared my opinion.

We went over the various events that had taken place at Buckworth with her, without learning anything new. Regarding Lethia Seagrave, her point of view coincided with Vivian's, perhaps even less favourable. If there was a noxious individual in the neighbourhood, it was the washerwoman's daughter.

'When we were children,' she explained, 'we sometimes played together. In those days, her wild and mysterious airs amused me. Then we lost sight of each other while we were studying. It never bothered me much that father used to visit her to have the cards read until I realised how very handsomely he had been paying her. At that time, before Vivian arrived, I was acting as his secretary. That's when I began to view her from a different angle and understand how much she benefitted from her reputation. Unfortunately for her, she was elbowed out by my new "mother", who is younger than me, by the way.'

All through her account, I noticed that our hostess's hands were becoming increasingly agitated and her speech was getting more rapid.

'I understand,' said Owen. 'Such situations are always delicate, at least at first. Generally one gets used to them.'

'Yes, and that's the danger. She knows what she's doing. She's succeeded in being accepted by everybody... including myself, I confess, despite being aware of her little game... Even my sister and her husband have succumbed. She's even exploited recent events to tighten the noose, in the name of family solidarity in the face of danger.'

'What danger? The White Lady?'

'Yes, but not only that. There are others.'

'You seem very anxious, madam.'

'How can I not be?' she retorted, her voice rising. 'There are threats from all sides at present. Over the last few months, the peace and quiet of our household has progressively been eroded by a string of events, each stranger than the one before. First there was that mysterious visitor my husband and I saw one night near the fountain. Then John's sudden "resurrection", as if back from the dead. Then the arrival of a secretary and her subsequent marriage to my father. Then the arrival of Margot and her newly found husband. Then the ghost that suddenly appeared in my father's bedroom, and the deadly prediction which later came true in the circumstances we all know. Don't you find all that a bit much, in the space of a mere three or four months?'

'Quite so,' I said, trying to placate her. 'But we're here to solve those mysteries.'

'And how do you plan to do that, exactly?'

Caught short, I turned to my friend, who replied after a moment.

'You've summarised the situation perfectly, madam. And also identified the danger, which does indeed appear to come from all sides. We shall be meeting the inspector, who has booked rooms for us at the inn, tonight, where we will put our heads together. It's a very complicated business, but we shall solve it, never fear.'

Before hearing Peter Corsham, who led us outside to the fountain, Owen confided that he was far from feeling the confidence he had exuded in the presence of his wife.

Starting from the fountain, the three of us walked diagonally across the leaf-strewn lawn as far as the wire fence which the mysterious visitor was supposed to have passed through as if it didn't exist.

After having described the event, he declared:

'It did happen a while back, however, around mid-June... I'd almost forgotten about it until people started talking about the White Lady again. So I'm not really sure about what I said. And I would be even less so, if Ann hadn't seen her as well.'

'So the fact she went through the fence like that was only an impression?' I asked.

'Try to imagine the scene. It was dark, I was close to the fountain and I saw her walk over here before she disappeared.'

'It would have been difficult to leap over it in a single bound,' observed Owen. 'It's over six feet high. And I can't see anywhere around where she could have hidden, except behind a tree, the nearest of which is thirty feet away... Do you remember seeing her on the other side?'

'I did get that impression, in fact. But, you know, sometimes you imagine certain things as the result of a sort of chain of ideas in your head.'

'That's the basic principle of illusion,' replied Owen. 'An illusion of which you were probably the victim. I have a couple of explanations in my head, but they both imply the presence of an accomplice. That said, this problem pales into insignificance compared to Miss Seagrave's troubling prediction, for example.'

After lighting a cigarette, Corsham proceeded to describe the facts of that encounter.

'My request for a horoscope was obviously a ruse. I went to see her as a guide, on behalf of our little community, to expose her schemes—but without my father-in-law's knowledge, of course. I confess not to have formed a clear opinion of her. It's as if there are two personalities in her... One with an almost touching naïveté and candour, and the other diametrically opposite, more calculating and astonishingly gifted... To be brief, after a relatively favourable horoscope for me, we started talking about the White Lady and her intentions. She made me pick a card from a special pack which used ancient symbols. I drew the jaguar. I can't remember her exact words, but she was categorical when she spoke of a predator on the prowl, which she compared to the White Lady on the point of choosing a new victim. The message could not have been clearer.'

Owen nodded thoughtfully, then asked:

'Was the card your personal choice? Could she have forced it on you by some subterfuge?'

'I don't think so,' replied Peter. 'After all, she could have told me the same thing if it had been a crocodile or a snake... or, better yet, compared the beast to a gentle cat and whispered happy news.'

'Of course,' agreed Owen smilingly.

'Be that as it may, I left with a feeling of apprehension, even though I was conscious of her little number. When I came back here, I made my report in a frivolous manner. I thought that if she really were the White Lady, she would never have had the gall to announce her next appearance. But I was wrong... There's no need to tell you of our distress when we learnt, a few days later, of the circumstances of young Harry's death.'

There was a long silence.

'Well, at least that point is now well-established,' declared Owen. 'The more we advance, the more each element of the puzzle gains in mystery. If things continue like this, I shall have to hand in my notice!' he added jovially.

'To each his profession,' replied Corsham.

'You're in insurance, I believe?'

'That's correct. I have an office in London. And the good luck to have a very competent deputy, because I don't go there every day. To be frank, I have the even better luck to have a rich father-in-law.'

'So insurance is not a vocation?'

'Absolutely not! I have other activities far more interesting. At the start of the war I worked in signals.'

As Owen frowned, he continued:

'Then in intelligence. I never suffered the same tribulations as John, but my work wasn't without risk. I admit to having gone soft since then.'

'So you're not from these parts?'

'Not at all. My father was Scottish and my mother Austrian. I obviously got my wartime assignment because I was bilingual.'

'I've lent a hand to the counter-espionage services in the past,' said Owen.'

'That would have been right up your street,' I joked. 'You love playing cat-and-mouse.'

That same evening, in the *Three Keys*, we discussed the situation with Inspector Lewis over a rustic meal.

'So,' he asked, 'is the profile of our White Lady becoming clearer?'

'Yes,' replied Burns. 'We established a list of suspects according to their physical characteristics. Ann Corsham is in first place, closely followed by Vivian Richards, with Margot in third, then Esther.'

'Their physical characteristics?' asked the policeman in astonishment. 'Are those your only criteria?'

'I'm sorry, but in this matter, they seem to be a major element. I can't imagine Sam over there in the role of our siren.' He indicated the landlord at the bar, who was built like a tank.

'That's all very well, but those are not the only elements... And did you forget young Seagrave? I would have expected her to be in the first three.'

'We haven't had time to see her. That's scheduled for tomorrow. We'll examine her thoroughly, I guarantee. From head to toe, with particular attention to her ankles, which are the source of grace in a woman, I think you will agree. Starting from this postulate, and the one which states that the White Lady is femininity personified, we believe that measuring all the suspects' ankles with the aid of a tape-measure will deliver us the White Lady on a plate.'

For a few seconds, the inspector looked at Owen as if he'd lost his marbles.

'You... you're joking, Mr. Burns?' he stammered.

'Of course! Because what else can we do, faced with this hodge-podge of growing mysteries? Particularly, as you yourself pointed out, there hasn't even been a crime yet. Just incomprehensible phenomena, outside the scope of a police investigation.'

'So what can we do?'

'I don't know. Maybe pray? That's what's generally recommended in desperate situations, isn't it?'

I couldn't believe it. My friend seemed to be giving up in advance in the face of an adversary beyond reach. But I had to agree. And the question of what to do next stared us cruelly in the face. The discussion which followed was more rational, but no more constructive, despite several rounds of beer. We left at around eleven, slightly the worse for wear, confident that the night would bring inspiration.

Once between the sheets, sleep hit me like a ton of bricks. At some point I vaguely heard a bell ring, but I went straight back to sleep. I was finally awakened by several violent knocks on the door. Before I could reply, it opened to reveal two familiar figures, Owen and Inspector Lewis.

'Get up, Achilles!' thundered the voice of my friend. 'We're going to the manor. There's been a new visit from the White Lady and they're in total panic.'

## 11

### The Dutch diamond merchant

*Achilles Stock's account (continued)*

*October 11*

At around two-thirty in the morning we found ourselves in the salon of Buckworth Manor, where the entire household had assembled, including the servants, Hildegard the cook, a plump woman with the look of an owl, and Janet, the maid, a thin girl of about twenty whose agonised expression summarised the general atmosphere of the place. Beforehand, we had met with Dr. Sanders, the village doctor who had been summoned urgently before anyone called the inn.

'More out of fear than sickness,' he told us before he left. 'Despite his age and weakness, Sir Matthew is a solid fellow. I gave him a couple of drops of digitalin and he's doing better. His heartbeat is back to normal. But this sort of thing mustn't be allowed to happen again. And I want to see him in my surgery in the not too distant future.'

This time, the White Lady had clearly targeted the lord of the manor. She had come to "find" him, just as she had done with little Harry, twice in the space of a quarter-of-an-hour of madness, which had finally ended with the intruder fleeing.

Seated in the corner of a sofa, wearing a wine-coloured dressing gown, Sir Matthew was putting on a brave face. His attempts to appear calm were betrayed by his ashen complexion. Vivian was sitting by his side, holding his hand. Her dark eyes had lost their confident look.

Before taking individual testimony from each of them, Inspector Lewis set about constructing the chronological sequence of events.

'At around midnight, you were all asleep in your respective beds on the floor above, and on the top floor for the servants. And that's when you heard a noise, Lady Richards.'

'Not exactly,' replied Vivian. 'I'd just woken up and sensed a presence in the room. A foreign presence. Matthew was sleeping soundly next to me. I woke him as gently as possible and explained to him, but he didn't fully react.'

'I pushed you away, in fact,' interjected her husband. 'But you insisted....'

'I lit the lamp... and my heart skipped a beat; she was facing us from the other side of the room! I let out a cry and that seemed to start her moving. She walked slowly towards Matthew with her hand raised.'

'By that time I was fully awake,' said her husband. 'Vivian hadn't dreamt it ... The damned creature had come back, more vindictive than before, and very close to me.'

'Was she smiling at you?'

'It's hard to say... Her arm was stretched out and her hand appeared excessively large... I was ice-cold with fright.'

'And you, madam, did you see her face?'

'Not at that moment... It was all happening so fast... To protect my husband, I seized the bedside lamp and brandished it in front of her, just like repelling monsters with fire.'

'And the lamp didn't go out?'

'No, luckily the cord was long enough. In any case, it worked... She backed away, then went around the bed to reach the door. She passed me whilst I was still brandishing the lamp, so I got a good look at her face... A face... I don't know how to describe it... Very beautiful, as white as her clothes, but terrifying... Her look froze me and I was completely paralyzed... I don't know whether it was deliberate, but as she passed she knocked the lamp out of my hand and extinguished it. I heard the door open, she went out, and we found ourselves in total darkness, in such a state of terror you can't imagine. Matthew was pressed against me and I wanted to call for help... But I was incapable of making a sound for a moment. Then I managed to let out a scream, so shrill that it must have woken everyone up.'

'I can confirm that,' said the major. 'Margot and I sat up in bed as one.'

'And shortly afterwards,' said Inspector Lewis, 'everyone but Sir Matthew was in the corridor, including you and the servants Hildegard and Janet, also alerted by the scream. Just after you'd heard

Lady Richards' explanation, and whilst her husband was still in bed, all the lights went out. That's when the situation degenerated into chaos. Everybody went to light candles, aided by the major who had rapidly gathered his torch.'

'That's right,' said John Peel with a grim smile. 'As an ex-military man I always sleep with it to hand. And, by the same token, I more or less took charge. Our White Lady fled, but where to? The first thing to do was to make sure she hadn't hidden somewhere on the same floor. At the same time, I asked Janet and Hildegard to check the fuse box in the cellar and replace any that had blown. Meanwhile Peter, who had found another torch, went with Vivian to the top floor to check that out. I naturally started with the small study, from which our nocturnal visitor had escaped the last time... During the next five to ten minutes, I have to admit the situation was very confused whilst we all wandered about by the light of candles and candelabra.'

'And during that time,' continued the inspector, turning to look at our host, 'the White Lady paid you a second visit.'

Sir Matthew nodded solemnly:

'Yes... I had barely recovered from my emotions and was still lying in bed when she came in. At first I thought it must be Vivian or one of my daughters. All I could see was a figure back-lit by the moving lights in the corridor. But her slow walk, her clothes, the shawl on her head, the hand extended in front... That's when I understood, and I thought of young Harry and his friends' accounts... My blood froze in my veins... I closed my eyes and shouted at the top of my lungs. That's all I remember.'

'We all heard the shout,' continued John Peel, 'without being able to locate where it came from. It could have been from any of the rooms in the corridor. Nevertheless, shortly afterwards I did see the back of someone in the corridor, at the top of the stairs, walking too assuredly in view of the circumstances. Moreover, she seemed to be still in her nightdress, whereas all our friends had put on dressing gowns. I was about thirty feet away from her. Then she turned around... With the shawl and the pale face, it could only be her. She reacted immediately and disappeared down the stairs.'

'And you, Mr. Corsham, you saw her just then as well. You were coming back down, accompanied by Lady Richards.'

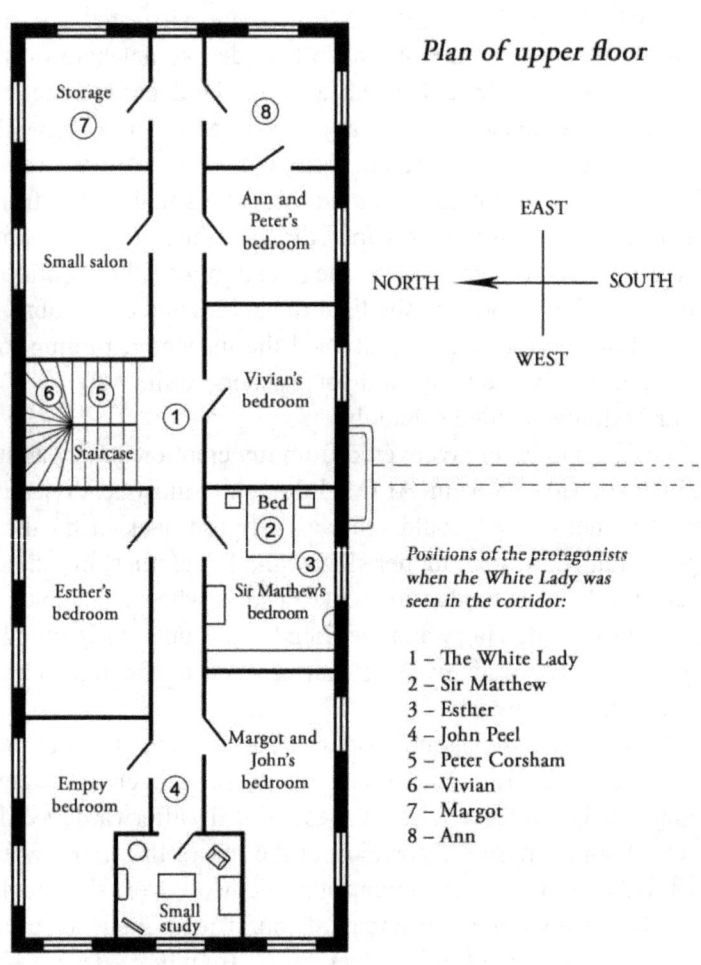

'Yes,' confirmed Peter. 'But I only realised when she started off and went rapidly down the stairs.'

'And you, my lady?'

'Yes... but I barely saw her. I was higher up, behind Peter.'

'Still at that same moment,' continued the policeman, consulting his notes, 'Esther was in Sir Matthew's bedroom, having just found him unconscious; Mrs. Peel was at the other end of the corridor in the storage room; and Mrs. Corsham was in her own bedroom.'

The three women nodded in silence.

'I didn't hesitate for long,' explained Peter, 'but John must have been quicker off the mark. He was almost level with me when I reached the landing. We went down the last few steps together... But there was no trace of the fugitive.'

'We scoured the hall with our torch lights,' continued John, 'trying to work out which direction to take. There was still no light, so I sent Peter to the cellar to look into it.'

Janet explained in embarrassment:

'Nothing worked. We located the fuse box and changed some of the fuses, but nothing happened, except sometimes there were sparks. Then, just before Mr. Corsham arrived, the lights went on again.'

'I was still in the hall when they came back on,' continued John Peel, 'but I had already detected a current of fresh air. That's when I noticed that the front door was slightly ajar. We went out and did a tour of the manor, but there was no one there, obviously. The fugitive had had plenty of time to get away. Meanwhile, Sir Matthew had regained consciousness. We immediately called the doctor and then the inn.'

There was a silence, then Ann addressed us with a piercing look in her eye:

'So now what do you plan to do, gentlemen?'

'Well,' said Lewis hesitantly, 'first of all, we'll go over the place with a fine-tooth comb to see what clues we can find.'

'And that's all? Don't you think the situation calls for stronger measures? This she-devil, whose appetite seems to grow with each appearance, seems to be able to come and go at will. Are you planning to wait with your arms folded for the next incident to happen?'

'No, of course not. I'm going to discuss it with my superiors.

Surveillance seems called for. Two officers on guard outside, starting at nightfall. What do you think, Burns?'

'A good idea,' agreed my friend. 'But I'd like to have a few words in private, if I may, Sir Matthew.'

After the rest of the household had retired, Owen posed his question:

'This business seems to be plunged in an impenetrable fog, but after what's just happened, the fog has dissipated a little. Of the four interventions of our White Lady, three have occurred here and converge more and more on you, Sir Matthew. Which leads us to a delicate question, but one of vital importance.'

The old man's face clouded over:

'So you think this creature wants to harm me personally?'

'Everything points to that conclusion, I'm afraid.'

'Then you believe in the legend?'

'That's a different matter. My question is the following: who would be interested to see you disappear?'

'Well....'

'Let's not beat about the bush. Who inherits your fortune?'

The lord of the manner shrugged his shoulders:

'My children, of course. And Vivian, whom I can't leave without protection. Not forgetting faithful Esther, although to a lesser extent.'

'That's all? No special bequests?'

'Yes, a few, but nothing large. I can't recite them all from memory. But to listen to you, one would think that the White Lady lives under this very roof... I may be mistaken, but don't the events of this difficult night prove the contrary?'

Owen avoided the question and looked his host straight in the eye:

'Have you any enemies, sir?'

'Enemies?' replied Sir Matthew with a bitter smile. 'Yes, and a lot of them. I spent quite a few years dealing in gold, diamonds and precious stones, and let me tell you, it's dog eat dog. There are winners and losers, and I was lucky enough to be amongst the former. As for the others, they all hate you! So, yes, undoubtedly I have a lot of enemies. That said, if any of them had wished me dead, they would have done it before now. All I do these days is mind my assets.'

'Don't they say that revenge is a dish best served cold?'

'Perhaps, but all that goes back a long way.'

'Think hard, Sir Matthew. One of them might be more motivated than the rest.'

The old man racked his brains whilst the flames in the hearth flickered, and slowly a smile came to his face.

'Yes, one name does stand out, even though he is no longer with us. Samuel Ziegler, a Dutch diamond merchant, my principal contact in Amsterdam. A trustworthy person, I thought, until I caught him cheating me. That's not done in the trade, and I discredited him. Discredited and disowned, he disappeared in cowardly fashion, but not before threatening my life.'

'When was this?'

'About ten years ago. He was fifty.'

'So roughly sixty today.'

'Yes, but I'm practically certain he's dead.'

'Why is that?'

'Because his wife committed suicide, which she had no reason to do otherwise. I've had many sleepless nights over it.'

'Did they have any children?'

'Yes, a girl and a boy, whose names I've forgotten. Neither of them turned out well, and if they're alive they would be in their twenties now—although I seem to remember the son died as well. It's an old story... But I'm feeling tired, gentlemen, and my doctor recommends rest, so if you will excuse me...,'

## 12

### In the backstreets of Buckworth

*Achilles Stock's account (continued)*

We got up in time for lunch. I was feeling the worse for wear, but the innkeeper's wife performed miracles. I felt much better after polishing off a succulent mushroom omelette accompanied by a pint of ale. At around two o'clock, whilst we were still at table, Inspector Lewis arrived. He hadn't had a wink of sleep, having supervised the search by reinforcements. Nevertheless, he was still functional, if not at his freshest.

'Nothing,' he declared, without further ado. 'We didn't turn up anything on any of the floors or the cellar. As for the power failure, that's just as likely to have been accidental as deliberate. It's not hard to trigger a short circuit at any outlet.'

'What about outside the manor?' I asked.

'Nothing there either. No clear footprints. And the grass on the lawn and the gravel on the paths don't help.'

'Have you asked for more reinforcements?' asked Owen, lighting a cigar.

'Of course, and the number of vigils will double, as of tonight. But frankly, I doubt that will enable us to catch our evil siren in our nets.'

'I agree, but it least has the merit of calming the souls inside the manor. By the way, have you contacted Scotland Yard about Ziegler?'

'Yes, they're looking into it,' said Lewis wearily.

'You don't appear to be enthused, my dear fellow.'

'Nothing enthuses me about this case, frankly. All the trails seem to lead nowhere. When I came here there was already the stench of a bog, but I never expected such a quagmire. Plus which, we eliminated quite a few suspects last night—or at least female suspects. According to the various testimonies and cross-checks, none of the three young women could have played the part of the White Lady, each of their husbands having furnished a solid alibi. Except Esther, and even there....'

'So what!' exclaimed Owen, blowing a long plume of smoke. 'That's a good thing, isn't it?'

'No. That leads us straight to Lethia Seagrave. She'll quickly take the blame in the village, you'll see. In fact, I think she's the one we should protect at this moment.'

'Aren't you indulging in favouritism?'

'I already told you, that girl hasn't had an easy life. I wouldn't want to have to handcuff her one day.'

'Well, we'll be questioning her this very afternoon. That's always been the plan. And there's the added advantage of learning what the future has in store for us, eh, Achilles?'

Whilst I shrugged my shoulders, Lewis nodded his approval.

'Perfect,' he said. 'Have a good time. As for me, even though my doctor hasn't prescribed it, I'm going to have a good long sleep, with your permission.'

\*\*\*

'That Harry was a rotten little trouble-maker, and nothing more. I'm not saying he deserved what he got, but he was far from an innocent victim.'

Lethia Seagrave had pronounced those words bluntly and with a vindictive gleam in her big brown eyes. At least she didn't beat about the bush, which could be attributed to rashness or naïveté. From the outset she had declared she had no alibi for the previous night. She had simply stayed home with her habitual companions, that's to say three cats, a dog, a rabbit and a crow. Naïve and rash maybe, but nonetheless perceptive:

'I know what you're thinking, gentlemen, and I could shock you even more by telling you I've even wished for his death. And I'm not the only one in the village. Ask the Wilsons, for example, whose son lost an eye due to a stupid joke gone wrong.'

Whilst she enumerated other faults of the little miscreant, I watched Owen out of the corner of my eye. He was clearly under her spell, and had been so since our arrival. It was almost as if he regarded her as a kindred spirit. After she had finished her indictment, he asked her if she had suffered any personal harm, and she pointed to the severed tail of one of the cats, which she was convinced was Harry's revenge for a severe admonition she had administered. After the two of them wandered off subject in a discussion about animals' feelings, he suddenly asked:

'Can we talk about your prediction of his tragic end?'

She shook her head.

'That's not exactly what I said.'

So saying, she described the details of her meeting with Peter Corsham, before concluding:

'He asked me about the possibility of a new manifestation of the White Lady. It was he who chose the jaguar card... And from that choice, decided by fate, he set the machinery underway. I imagine he announced the dark omen to those around him, and it spread to the village. It reached Harry's ears and gave him the idea to drag his friends to the pond that night, with fatal consequences.'

'It's disconcerting,' said Owen, examining his fingernails. 'Each gesture, each interaction can modify the course of events... Each word also....'

'So be very careful about the question you're about to ask,' laughed the young woman.

'And you about your answers, miss. I come back to our White Lady and what is whispered about her. You can't ignore it, can you?... So my question is, what do you think of the rumours? Is there any basis or not?'

Lethia's face clouded over.

'Before me, it was my mother who was subject to the same suspicions. Worse, even. Because she had turned the heads of several of the villagers, others saw in her the incarnation of evil, in other words, a witch. Even though the legends of the "night washerwoman" or of the White Lady go back a long way, you must have been told about them... In fact, my mother suffered from a strange malady, which she transmitted to me. I can assure you that I've been cured, however... Can you guess what it was, Mr. Burns? It's a sickness no one wants to talk about... one which draws you out into the night...'

'You were both sleepwalkers?'

'Yes,' she confirmed solemnly. 'And it's not an agreeable feeling to wake up suddenly in the middle of the night, in a nightdress in a deserted street, and wonder what you are doing there.'

'And you've never told anyone?'

'Yes, at the beginning. But no one listened, as usual, preferring to treat me as a guilty party looking for excuses. I resigned myself to the situation, given my mother's reputation, my isolation, my "strange" attraction to animals, and—to cap it all—my fortune-telling sessions. All that contributed to my aura of mystery and my reputation as a strange woman with "supernatural powers". So much so that I just kept quiet.'

'But you must realise that, in the current climate, that reputation is very prejudicial.'

'I know. But I've done nothing to be ashamed of. And I'm well protected.'

'Ah! By whom?'

Smiling, and holding Owen's look with those big brown eyes, she replied:

'Why, by the White Lady herself, of course! Only she has the power to put an end to our time on this earth.'

'Be careful what you say, miss. You know the importance of words. Regarding your past affliction, who in the village knows about it? Or rather, who took you seriously?'

She shrugged.

'I don't really know... Maybe just Sir Matthew.'

'Ah! I was forgetting. He was one of your regular clients, from what we've been told. And generous into the bargain.'

'It's true. He's very rich, but not mean.'

'Otherwise, what do you think of him?'

The young woman appeared embarrassed, but Owen persisted:

'You must know him pretty well, after all those séances. You've had ample opportunity to probe his soul.'

After a long silence, during which she stroked the cat, she replied:

'There are two personalities inside him, one good, the other bad. I know that's a very basic way to put it, but that's how I see him. And I'm going to stop there, gentlemen, because I'm not one to judge.'

My friend and I exchanged glances whilst Lethia continued to stroke the cat.

'We've also been told you practice automatic handwriting,' continued Owen.

'What has that to do with the investigation?'

'Nothing. It's a personal interest. I just have trouble understanding the principle, or rather the results.'

'It's another one of my gifts,' she replied simply. 'But I don't derive any financial benefit from it, I just do it for relaxation, to discover more about my subconscious, or read unknown stories from my own hand. I have no literary pretentions, in fact.'

Turning to look at a shelf full of books, Owen recommenced:

'I see some jewels of English literature here.'

'Yes, I started to study for an arts degree.'

'At Oxford?'

'Yes, but I didn't complete it.'

'Lack of funds, I presume?'

'No... in fact, yes. It was too much to ask of mummy. She'd already sacrificed enough.'

Her sudden reversal had not escaped our notice, and she knew it. Owen changed the subject:

'I've also heard about your salon in London, which apparently is doing well.'

'I'm not complaining.'

'Do you go there often?'

'Usually the consultations are by appointment, which I try to group together. Usually I go there twice a week. But if you're interested, we could do a séance here.'

'Why not?' replied Owen cheerfully. 'I'll think about it. Visiting you in your official lair would be equally suitable. One last thing, regarding your automatic writing. You've intrigued me. Would it be inconvenient to let me have an example?'

Lethia seemed amused.

'Not at all. But I need to sort my papers out first. And you might be disappointed.'

Owen laid on the charm:

'Disappointed by you, miss? Forgive my impertinence, but that's hard to imagine.'

After taking leave of Lethia, we took a stroll around the backstreets of Buckworth. Owen wanted to absorb the atmosphere of the village, "all the better to penetrate its secrets," he explained. Behind each door and each window, he sniffed out their ancient secrets. The Tudor-style cottages attracted the most attention.

'Can you sense the vibrations emanating from these old stones, Achilles?' he asked. 'They want to send us a message; they witnessed the birth of the White Lady... They are witnesses of the first order.' He breathed in deeply. 'Even the air is impregnated with the smells of the past.'

'You should try clairvoyance yourself, Burns!'

'And why not?'

'So, is the light of truth about to break through?'

'Yes, but little by little, like a simmering stew.'

He pointed to a red brick building in a dilapidated state:

'That's the Lewis family home. He told me he was hoping to renovate it.'

'Well, he'd better put in some overtime, then!'

'Achilles, for heaven's sake, please lose that habit of only seeing the material aspect of things.'

'And you stop beating about the bush. What are you trying to achieve here? Do I have to remind you that we have a serious problem on our plate? And there you were, strutting like a peacock in front our chief suspect. Don't deny it!'

'Didn't it occur to you that it was a manoeuvre, the better to get at the truth?'

'So, is she the White Lady?'

He stopped suddenly, a finger to his lips.

'I think Miss Seagrave plays a part in this mystery. But what kind? That of an instigator, or a victim? The whole question is there.'

Inspector Lewis was not there waiting for us on return, nor did he turn up for dinner. The landlord told us he had not left his room. Afterwards, Owen announced that he needed to take a nocturnal stroll to get his thoughts in order, and since he didn't invite me to come along, I deduced that he wanted to be alone.

What was he hoping for? To meet the White Lady?

A few minutes after he left, I put on my coat and left the hotel in turn. My intention was not to follow him, but just to stretch my legs as well. Once outside, I regretted my decision. The night was particularly damp. Only a few lights were on in the windows. I was thankful I had brought along my little torch. After wandering haphazardly through the streets, I ended up in front of the church, which I found somewhat reassuring, as if the religious edifice had the power to dispel demons... In truth, I was scared stiff. The damp darkness penetrated my soul insidiously, inflaming my imagination as I tried to review all the elements of the affair. As if attracted by a flame, I found myself walking in the direction of the manor, which seemed to be at the heart of the problem.

Five minutes later I saw the wire fence of the property. It occurred to me that the two policemen assigned by Inspector Lewis would be on duty outside the building. It was not the moment to be detected and create a false alarm. I made my way cautiously along the fence, looking for a suitable observation post. Eventually, a gap between the trees allowed me to distinguish a good part of the manor. Several windows on the upper floor were illuminated. I stood there for several long minutes feeling the cold encroaching and asking myself why I was there: was it in the secret hope of witnessing another drama?

Suddenly something moved at the foot of the building... One shape and then another, no doubt the two policemen. They seemed to be exchanging a few words... As my eyes became accustomed to the darkness I could distinguish their capes and helmets, which I found reassuring. But that is when a third shape, roughly halfway between them and me... Someone lying in wait like me... I was overcome by a growing wave of anxiety. The shape was neither white, nor feminine. Eventually I managed to identify it by its clothing and its bearing: my friend Owen! What the devil was he doing there? Giving a hand with the vigil? Or checking on the effectiveness of their surveillance? Whatever the reason, I could hardly send him a signal without attracting the attention of the police officers.

I started retracing my footsteps. The explanations could wait for when we were back in the warm comfort of the inn. I was planning to go there directly, but at the principal crossroads of the village, I hesitated. The road to the south led to the clearing in the woods and thence to the path opening onto the pond. I don't know what possessed me to do so, but I chose to take the detour. I needed my torch occasionally in order to find my way, but I used it sparingly, as I was worried about being detected. It was absurd, because there was no one there except the inhabitants of the woods.

Arriving at the destination, I looked at the pond under the silver light of a crescent moon. There was something magical about the place, where even the slightest sound to disturb the deep silence seemed to resonate endlessly. I stood there immobile for a while, ill at ease but fascinated, thinking about the tragic circumstances of young Harry's death. It must have been a night like this one... I sensed the cold numbing my limbs but not my mind. Each scene of the tragedy, as described by the children, unfolded clearly in my head. The discovery of the fox trap... the torn stems of hemlock... the tree stump... the apparition of the White Lady....

At that moment, there was no need to force my imagination to see her arriving behind my back. I turned around, as if by reflex. No white shape, fortunately. But no absolute darkness either! For a brief moment, I thought I saw a reflection far away on the path... Sensing my pulse accelerate, I stood motionless, scanning the darkness. Something was moving... Something was coming towards me... A glacial shudder ran down my spine.

## 13

## "The Star of the Shadows"

The door opened suddenly and Vivian came into the salon, a gloomy look on her face.

'A breeze accompanied by lightning,' commented Peter Corsham, leaning against the mantelpiece, a glass of whisky in his hand.

'Excuse me?' she said, her face flushed.

'You seem more lively and more upset than usual'

'Upset,' she said through gritted teeth. 'Who wouldn't be at a time like this?'

Her wrathful gaze fell in turn on Peter, then on Ann and Margot, sharing the sofa, and finally on John, who was leafing through a newspaper.

'On top of which, it's not very pleasant to be ogled when one's in the bathroom.'

'What are you talking about?' asked Ann.

'Those two policemen who are supposed to protect us. Well, at least one of them... I almost came face-to-face with him when I opened the window. There was nothing left to the imagination! But I'll get my own back, you'll see.'

'Don't be too hard on him,' said Peter. 'Think of it as a reward for the poor fellow obliged to spend the whole night under the stars.'

'Well, that's reassuring. Anyway, you can serve me a glass of sherry.'

After Peter had obliged, she continued:

'Speaking of surveillance, I don't think it's very effective. All it does is put us more on edge. As if we needed that!'

'In other words,' said Ann coldly, 'you reproach me for my initiative.'

'I never said that. I'm simply assessing the situation... in view of the new developments.'

'Which are...?'

Vivian lit a cigarette before replying:

'Well, according to Matthew, the police are on a new track, involving personal revenge. It's no secret that he's made a few enemies over time.'

'Hmm....' mused Major Peel. 'So the enemy came from the outside. Well, at least that has the merit of clarifying the situation.'

'All we need to do is identify her,' added Peter. 'Has the old man any ideas? Who, amongst his old enemies, has the physique of our graceful night visitor? Of that young and pretty White Lady who has come to haunt him for his past misdeeds?'

'Yes,' agreed Vivian. 'Matthew has his suspicions. An old work colleague. But obviously there's incompatibility with regard to age and physical appearance.'

John shook his head pensively:

'We've been blinded by the White Lady, and that's a mistake. I think that's bait that has been dangled in front of us, exploiting the local legend. The question of her identity is secondary, because she's obviously a paid accomplice, some circus acrobat or light-fingered gypsy. In other words, the police should be looking for the one pulling the strings.'

'I agree, darling,' replied Margot, coming out of her reverie. 'But in that case, it must be a very elaborate plan, put together several months ago, well before your return. Because, let me remind you, the first appearance occurred back in the beginning of the summer.'

'That's right,' agreed her sister. 'And what's just as bizarre is that her "visits" were not all concentrated on father. I'm thinking of the one to the pond in particular.'

'Good observation, darling,' declared Peter. 'Not only did it not happen here, but the action there was sudden... and fatal.'

'The children exaggerated, that's all,' chimed in John. 'Pure logic rejects any other hypothesis.'

'The famous male logic! It's either black, or it's white. Personally, I don't find the logical course of events as logical as all that.'

'Maybe not,' retorted John. 'But at least we know now that the enemy comes from outside. And if you need additional proof, we found the front door ajar that night... But where's Matthew, in fact? Has he already gone to bed?'

'I don't think so,' replied Vivian, 'but I'll check.'

A few moments later she found her husband in his ground floor office, crouched over the table, illuminated by a lamp with a green shade—the only source of light, apart from the flames in the hearth.

'You should get some rest, darling,' she said solicitously.

'Rest? I've been doing nothing else all day!'

'So come and join us in the salon.'

'With pleasure, but I just have to finish something.'

She gave him a gentle kiss on the forehead.

'In that case, darling, I'll leave you. But don't take too long. And don't forget your doctor's recommendations.'

As the door closed behind his young wife, a tender smile came to his face. It was as if he were thanking fate for having put such a gentle creature in his path. Getting up, he went over to a safe concealed behind a removable section of shelving. After activating the combination, he withdrew a small wooden chest and spread the contents out over the table. Coloured flashes of light were reflected in his eyes as he gleefully observed his collection of precious stones.

Some were uncut, some were finely polished, but each prompted a recollection. Some, like the lapis-lazuli, represented business successes; others, like the magnificent small ruby, represented failures. He picked up a small diamond, given to him by his one-time friend, Sam Ziegler.

Overcome with remorse, he felt a lump rising in his throat. His revenge was disproportionate, he told himself, but Ziegler had started it by betraying him. He was responsible in large part for what had happened to his wife and children afterwards, particularly little Deborah. Poor child... After the death of her parents, she had disappeared into the abyss. He had hired a private detective to find her in order to save her and offer her financial aid, but it was a human wreck that had been found in the ports of Hamburg. A wreck with an unrecognisable face who had reached the lowest depths of degradation. He would never forget the moment she spat in his face, pure hatred in her eyes, as if the mere sight of him disgusted her....

His eye fell on what he considered to be the jewel of his collection: "The Star of the Shadows," a magnificent pale blue sapphire, which owed its name to the long series of misfortunes which had befallen its previous owners, the purchase of which he had kept secret. Each time he contemplated it, he had a curious and indefinable expression. There was something glacial in its colour, the blue of mountain lakes.

The stone, renowned for its powers of lucidity or clairvoyance, seemed to want to transmit a message. It seemed to vibrate at his touch, and an icy current travelled up his spine. But its sinister reputation could not be the cause. Numerous times he had tried to pierce its secret by shining a light on it, so far in vain. But now, in light of recent events, the veil of mystery was starting to lift. With the revealing text he had read recently, and the various manifestations of the White Lady... The message could not be clearer: his end was rapidly approaching. He would soon have to pay for his sins....

Sir Matthew turned the sombre thoughts over in his mind without emotion. It was in the order of things.

A slight sound outside made him jump. He went over to the window and noticed crunching noises on the gravel. He shrugged. It was obviously the night guard on their rounds. He smiled ironically. As if those brave policemen could change the course of events! Their presence was perfectly useless.

He came back to the table to contemplate "The Star of the Shadows" once more. A white, vaporous shape seemed to move inside the bluish brightness of the stone... Its face became clearer... A beautiful, smiling face as white as snow, which he knew only too well.

## 14

### Cherchez la femme

*Achilles Stock's account (continued)*

*October 12*

'... That thing that I had seen moving, and which approached slowly along the path... You may laugh, but at that moment, I could have sworn it was the White Lady! But I eventually recognised the figure... of my friend Owen!'

Inspector Lewis was having trouble hiding his amusement after hearing my account of the trip to the pond. We hadn't seen him since the previous day. He'd left the inn in the morning, was still absent at midday, and it was only in the late afternoon that he had reappeared, happy to take a break and discuss the situation over a pint of ale.

'I had a similar experience,' said Owen. 'I had gone to take a look at the manor to get an idea of the efficiency of the operation you had put in place. I began by breaching the wire fence without being noticed. And your officers didn't notice either, when I went closer to spy on them. And I'm not talking about the surrounding darkness, nor the trees and bushes on the boundaries of the manor. In short, I quickly formed the impression that an intruder would have no difficulty getting into the manor, via a badly shut window, or one of the service entrances, if they had a skeleton key or a duplicate. On the other hand, I didn't notice Achilles arrive... I retraced my steps after his departure and, just as he did, I decided to visit the pond, to get an idea of the scene of the crime at night. I have to say my state of concentration was optimal, with the forest air, the freshness of the night, and the surrounding darkness. I had to switch my torch on a few times to guide myself along the path, and that's what must have caught Achilles' attention. And I, in turn, noticed a figure frozen by the side of the pond, whose surface glistened under the light of the moon. How could I not have thought of *her* at that moment? Of the

White Lady whom we had been tracking? Nevertheless, one part of me refused to believe it... I forced myself to approach the figure slowly, just to be absolutely sure... And it was only then that I recognised my friend's massive silhouette.'

Lewis, who had just finished his beer, shook his head in amusement.

'Well, gentlemen, for two experts with your reputation, I don't know what to say. I hadn't realised you were as impressionable as schoolgirls!'

'That might actually be our trump card, inspector,' replied Owen amusedly. 'That frame of mind allowed us to better appreciate the atmosphere of the place, and of the village, after dark. To understand that, in such an environment, where the very stones murmur the ancient past, the natives are inclined towards fantasies of the imagination.'

'Wait a minute!' exclaimed the policeman, frowning. 'Are you telling me that Billy and Jack were just hallucinating?'

'No. Particularly since I had the opportunity to listen to little Jack that very morning. His version did not vary one inch from what we know. However—and this is the lesson of last night—one detail, one element misinterpreted from the start, can change the whole of a story. That's the principle of mistaken identity, in fact. Or reading. You identify a word by its context or by a few key letters. Your conditioned mind doesn't bother to decrypt each character. I believe Jack and Billy are firmly convinced about what they saw, or thought they saw... And, as we have just experienced, in the murky atmosphere hanging over that pond at night, it doesn't require much for your senses to become weakened and your perception altered.'

'But they firmly declared having seen a woman all in white placing her hand on Harry to deliver the final blow.'

'I prefer not to go into the details for now, inspector. Just remember the principle, which can equally apply to the apparitions of the White Lady in the manor. I repeat, that experience, which caused you so much mirth, was very fruitful.'

'Oh, very well,' replied Lewis resignedly. 'We don't actually know any more for it, but we've been warned. Meanwhile, you haven't told me about your visit to Lethia. What did you learn?'

Owen briefly covered our meeting with the young woman, then

asked:

'Were you aware, inspector, of her and her mother's somnambulism?'

The policeman stroked his moustache as he shook his head.

'No, but I can check into it. But I don't see that it helps her much. People will just see confirmation of their views. To be more practical, is she or is she not a potential culprit, in your eyes?'

'For my part,' I interjected, 'I would say yes. In any case, that girl is by no means the simpleton some make her out to be.'

'That's certainly true,' agreed Owen, 'but I would be more nuanced, Achilles, far more nuanced. If Miss Seagrave were to be guilty of such a scheme, she would be the instigator rather than the executor. The person who sowed panic the other night in the manor showed great agility, audacity and sang-froid. Miss Seagrave possesses all those qualities, in addition to being very supple....'

I interrupted with a wink to Lewis:

'My friend didn't fail to take her measurements with a tape measure.'

'I see,' said the inspector. 'She's captivated you, Burns. Is that it?'

'I have to say she's an interesting suspect, who merits further investigation.'

'Owen plans to visit her in London for a private reading of the cards,' I mocked.

My friend turned to look at me:

'So, Achilles, are you jealous?'

Lewis cleared his throat:

'Come, gentlemen, let's be serious. What were you saying, Burns?'

'Simply that I don't see her in the role of the impetuous White Lady that I've just described. Wandering in the streets with a mystic air, maybe, but playing the role of an impulsive phantom, no. And what reason would she have to terrorise Sir Matthew?'

The policeman nodded his head with a curious smile, and declared:

'That was my point of view, Mr. Burns. But I've changed my opinion since.'

'Since last night?'

'Yes, I was at the manor today, and I learnt a few things. According to Ann, Miss Seagrave's name appeared in his will. His old will, that is, because he's changed it since his second wedding. That's the first point. The second is that I've just received information about Miss Seagrave's bank account. And I was frankly surprised. I thought she was in straitened circumstances, but it turns out that she's accumulated quite a tidy sum over the last few years. Her soothsaying activities are far more lucrative than I thought. There are a number of cheques from notable people, such as Sir Matthew, whom we already knew about.'

'And so?' asked Owen. 'If he treated her so generously, why would Lethia want to kill the goose that laid the golden eggs?'

Lewis pulled a face:

'I don't really know, because the situation has changed substantially since Sir Matthew's remarriage.'

'For everyone, it seems to me,' retorted Owen. 'And for the worse, except for Vivian, obviously.'

'Speaking of whom,' continued the inspector, grinning, 'she complained this morning about one of our watchmen, who apparently took advantage of his position to ogle her through the bathroom window. The officer in question denied it vigorously. It seems that our surveillance is more of an inconvenience than anything else. Sir Matthew himself says it doesn't serve any useful purpose. I don't know why, but he gave me a curious impression whilst he was talking. And if we add in your own conclusion, Mr. Burns, I'm starting to think we should put an end to it. What do you think?'

Owen had raised his hand to call for silence. After a moment's thoughtful reflection, he replied:

'What I think is that you're right in thinking Sir Matthew's recent marriage shook the peace and calm of the household and led to the events which followed... But there's something that doesn't fit.'

'What?'

'There's a small problem with the chronology. Trivial, but enough to undermine everything.'

We didn't learn any more. As was his custom, Owen kept the fruit of his cogitations to himself. The art of uttering mystifying words must have started when he first learnt to speak.

*October 20*

A whole week had passed without the White Lady drawing attention to herself. We had gone up to the capital the day after our last meeting with Lewis, who had quickly resumed his normal functions in Oxford. The investigation had stalled, and to pursue it under such circumstances would have been pointless. That morning we saw our old friend Superintendent Wedekind at Scotland Yard. According to him, he was in possession of new information. Frank Wedekind still had his brigand's moustache and thick eyebrows but they were now quite gray, and he had started to think about retirement. But, as always, his sombre expression lit up whenever he smiled. Which it did as soon as he saw us.

'Well, hello my friends. Your sojourn in the country has been beneficial, by the looks of it.'

'You should have come with us,' replied Owen. 'You would have gained a few springtimes.'

'I have to tell you that the harvest hasn't been great. But, quite frankly, I knew that already. Lewis has been on the phone, and it appears you haven't caused any sparks to fly.'

'That's true. But we're carnivores and we haven't found any red meat to sink our teeth into.'

'Still as biting as ever, Burns,' retorted Wedekind, lighting a cigar. 'Wasn't there anything suspicious about the death of the kid by the pond?'

'I'm sure Lewis must have spoken to you about it. It was a case of accidental poisoning. We all looked for some other explanation, but in vain. That's if you exclude the story of the phantom.'

The superintendent nodded his head and retrieved a file from the stack on his desk.

'Nothing sensational from our side, but you never know. Searches always take a long time, but I must say our Dutch colleagues were very responsive. I'll start with the case of Andrew Moog, a thirty-year-old thug, suspected of theft and fraud, but never convicted. The problem is, he left the area nearly ten years ago, and has not been seen since. No word about him on the rest of the continent and no reports about him from frontier guards, unless he's changed his identity. Frankly, I think the young wife has been having you on.'

'We do too, Wedekind, I can assure you.'

'What now? Someone tries to frighten a rich old man who's been conned into placing a ring on a young filly's finger? Cherchez la femme, find out who profits, and you'll know who....'

'Of course. But it's a dubious hypothesis. In the first place, Lady Richards has a solid alibi for the night when the White Lady made her first appearance at the manor. According to her husband and one of his sons-in-law. Furthermore, our lovely Vivian didn't tie the knot until after the White Lady's first apparition.'

'Ah! Now I understand,' I exclaimed. 'That's the chronological problem you were talking about!'

'Yes, amongst others, Achilles. Full marks for your excellent memory. Unless she prepared her plan before meeting him, which would be banking heavily on her powers of seduction, formidable though they are. Speaking of which, have you had time to delve into her past?'

'A little. It must be said that Miss Vivian Marsh has had a bumpy past. Even so, it seems to conform to her declarations, at least as far as the English and French parts are concerned. It would seem to me that your second idea of revenge for past injustices is the more fruitful one to explore. And I can tell you that the Ziegler case is not without interest... A very sad affair, in fact.

'Let's start in 1914. Ruined, Sam Ziegler vanished, and there's good reason to think that he bought his own ticket to paradise. In despair, his wife threw herself out of a high window. But you knew that already. The couple had two children, a boy and a girl, Cornelius and Deborah, who were twenty-five and eighteen at the time.

'Cornelius was severely wounded during a bombardment in Belgium. After he left hospital, in good shape, he disappeared, only to turn up four years later. He was a crew member on the "Tiger", a merchant sea vessel which was wrecked on the Moroccan coast on November 27, 1918, to be exact. Foundering on the rocks, the vessel tipped over and disgorged its contents, merchandise and crew, on the beach. There were no survivors, but Cornelius's body was never found. Did he escape, by some miracle? That's the question, even though one might ask, if that were the case, why he didn't turn up afterwards.

'Now let's move on to Deborah. She was very shaken by what

happened to her parents, and even spent a short time in a psychiatric hospital. Afterwards, she became a prostitute. After losing trace of her, she reappeared in the Hamburg dockyards with a local pimp. After that, no trace of her. A very sad story.'

'Quite,' agreed Owen. 'Sad from a human standpoint, but rich in possibilities for our investigation. It's clear that if one of them survived, their hatred for Sir Matthew—the man who destroyed their family—would justify even the most diabolical plan of revenge.'

'Exactly,' said Wedekind, with a crooked smile. 'And, if my calculations are correct, Deborah would be twenty-eight today and Cornelius thirty-five.'

'Food for thought,' observed Owen. 'What do you think, Achilles?'

'I know what you're thinking,' I responded, unable to hide the excitement in my voice. Where is the possible survivor hiding today? Behind which mask?'

'Continue, my friend. I can see you're inspired.'

'If we start with Cornelius, there are two possibilities. First, there's Peter Corsham, who admitted to having a chequered past. Then John Peel. They're both the right age, but only a detailed search of their past will enable us to deduce more.'

'Right. Wedekind will take care of that. Now, what if it were Deborah who survived?'

'That's a bit more delicate, even though the age matches all our candidates for the White Lady. I think we can safely eliminate Sir Matthew's two daughters. It's hard to believe that a substitution would have escaped their father's notice. And we can rule out Vivian for the same reason. If she was Deborah, he would have recognised her. That leaves the last of the lot. And there, I have to be more prudent.'

'If you're thinking of Lethia, you can eliminate her, just as you eliminated Vivian.'

'Not necessarily. First of all, she left the village for a long time, ostensibly to pursue her studies. Deborah could have taken her place at some point, particularly since Lethia's mother passed away during that period.'

'Yes, but as far as Sir Matthew is concerned, the problem hasn't changed.'

'But it has! And it would explain the attention he lavished on her.

Deborah didn't hide what she had done—justified by who knows what excuse—and spun him a poignant yard along the lines of:

"I used to hate you more than any other human being, but I've known you were generous at heart..." And, given her experience in Germany, one can well imagine she could add a carnal argument to shore up her little comedy.'

'You're more Machiavellian than I thought, Achilles. But I do admit you have a point. We need to refine the analysis. I'm sure Wedekind won't mind adding a few hours to his forty years of loyal service.'

'The hours are starting to build up,' groused the superintendent. 'I don't know whether you realise, but fishing in the past costs a lot of manpower. And our London criminals aren't going to go on strike whilst we're doing it!'

The following morning, whilst we were partaking of a late breakfast, I made it known to Owen that I needed to give serious consideration to returning to Wedgewood, where the business required my presence. He was about to reply when the telephone rang in reception.

Owen got up to take the call. When he returned a few moments later, it was to announce lugubriously:

'I'm afraid you're going to have to postpone your return, my dear friend. That was Inspector Lewis: our White Lady has made another appearance at the manor. A new visit to Sir Matthew, which was almost his last: he came within inches of losing his life.'

## 15

**The crow's feather**

*Achilles Stock's account (continued)*

*October 23*

The inspector had made it clear that we would have to await Sir Matthew's release from hospital before questioning him, which is why we didn't go to Buckworth until the following day. And it wasn't until early afternoon on Thursday that we saw the lord of the manor in the salon. He greeted us with a pale smile, his face visibly marked by the recent events. A silk scarf knotted around his neck seemed to underscore his fragility.

'Yes, gentlemen, I really thought that judgment day had arrived,' he confided. 'A terrifying cold gripped me when she placed her hands on my chest and my heart, and I lost consciousness. And when I came to, it was the face of my doctor that I saw. He seemed very worried.'

'I don't suppose you have an idea of the exact time,' asked Owen.

'No. It all happened so suddenly... It was well into the night, but it could equally well have been midnight or four o'clock. Apparently, it was around five o'clock that Esther found me unconscious.'

'And you went to bed alone at ten, with your wife in her own bedroom.'

'Yes, I was a bit restless. But from now on she's decided not to let me sleep alone.'

'Do you remember anything special about your bedroom before you went to sleep?'

'No. I took my medicine, including a sleeping-pill, from the bedside table and went to sleep, without reading as I normally do. All I can remember after that is having a nightmare. I was walking under an oppressive sun, in an intolerable furnace... Then I was walking in snow, lashed by a glacial wind, fighting against the elements in intense cold... That's when I woke up in the familiar surroundings of my bedroom, but still with the sensation of cold... That's when I saw her, in the same place as always, at the other end of the bed, facing me and smiling.'

'Was the light on?'

'Not the lamp. I think there was a candle on the console, but it's only an impression. There wasn't much light, but it was enough to identify her, with her white dress and shawl around her head, and her face, beautiful and strange at the same time.'

'Was the window open?'

'Yes, I got that impression. But it was all so sudden I can't be sure. All I saw was her, staring at me with those frightening eyes, whilst she came towards me with outstretched hands. I lay paralyzed in my bed, covered in sweat and shivering from cold, with my pyjama top fully open. The cold continued to intensify as her hands got closer, and when she placed them on my chest it was like a violent electric shock. Then the black hole....'

'Between that moment and the time of her apparition, would you say ten seconds elapsed?'

Sir Matthew paused for reflection:

'Not even that. She started coming at me the moment I saw her... In any case, I've come back from very far away, gentlemen.'

'That's only an impression, according to medical advice,' observed Owen. 'Right now, you need to summon all your courage and all your forces.'

'Why do you say that, Mr. Burns?' asked the old man, with an inscrutable look.

My friend seemed taken aback. He mumbled:

'Why, to continue to stay alive.'

A peaceful smile appeared on Sir Matthew's face:

'Someone has decided otherwise, it appears. And I'm afraid, Mr. Burns, that despite all your talent you cannot stop the wheels of the Great Watchmaker.'

There was a silence, then Owen asked:

'Do you remember our last discussion about the Dutch diamond merchant Ziegler?'

'Of course. And I can tell you I've thought about him many times since.'

'It's about his daughter, Deborah.'

'Have you had any news?'

'No. But I was wondering whether you would still be able to recognise her?'

He thought for a moment before replying:

'Let me see, it goes back quite a long time. But I think so.'

'Could you describe her?'

'She was a beautiful adolescent, with long chestnut hair, which she inherited from her mother. A pleasant face with expressive eyes, but no special features... Ah! I understand. You think she might be the White Lady, come back to take her revenge. Is that it?'

'It's one hypothesis out of many,' replied my friend tactfully.

Sir Matthew shook his head slowly.

'I think you're barking up the wrong tree, Mr. Burns, and that the explanation of the mystery will not come from logical deduction.'

After taking our leave, we rejoined Inspector Lewis, who had been waiting for us in the hall, and went up to Sir Matthew's bedroom with him.

'The facts are relatively straightforward. At around five in the morning, Esther, unable to sleep, got up to make coffee for herself in the kitchen. Passing in front of this room, she detected a slight current of air which she quickly realised was coming from under the door. She was puzzled, because Sir Matthew never sleeps with the window open at this time of year. After knocking softly without getting a response, she opened the door to take a look. The window was wide open, just as she had anticipated, and her employer was lying bizarrely on the bed, his face a purplish colour and his pyjama top unbuttoned.

'You could say she saved his life, for if they'd found him an hour later, he would no longer be of this world. She called an ambulance and Dr. Sanders, who found that his heart was only beating feebly. Sir Matthew had been victim of a massive heart attack. For how long, nobody knew, but in any case, not more than three hours. At the Oxford hospital he had been taken to urgently, the early diagnosis was not optimistic. We now know he survived, but not without serious repercussions affecting his life style. No further excesses of any kind.

'Nobody noticed any strange noises during the night. Everyone claims to have slept soundly, including Miss Seagrave, who was in her own home. So no one has an alibi, with the possible exception of the two couples. But each of them could have sneaked out without being noticed by their spouse.'

Owen gave a cursory look around the room, and asked:

'Did you find anything out of the ordinary here?'

'No, unless you count the blob of wax on the console from the lighted candle.'

'I find that wide open window very curious, as if to indicate the route taken by our nocturnal visitor. You've checked the ground below, I assume?'

'Of course. But come and check it yourself.'

Ten minutes later, we were looking up at the window from the gravel path as Lewis continued his explanations:

'As you can see, the manor is perfectly maintained, which is unfortunate in a way. A few patches of moss would have helped. We haven't found any suspicious patches, but that doesn't rule out the possibility of acrobatics. It wouldn't be very difficult for someone agile. The mullioned window opposite us, situated immediately below the one of interest, has a frame which juts out, capped by a thick lintel. It only needs a ladder to reach, and from there it would be possible to hoist oneself to the window above, agreed?'

'Absolutely. But what I don't understand is why our intruder complicated matters, when she's always had easy access to the manor.'

'I know, Burns. Up until now, I've limited myself to the bare facts, but between you and me, I urged Sir Matthew to have the locks changed on the entrance doors. I had to insist. Eventually he agreed, but it was as if he'd yielded to a fantasy on my part.'

'I see. We've also noticed a strange resignation on his part, as if he's ready to follow the White Lady on her next visit. It looks as if the enemy's aggression has borne fruit.'

'Yes, alas!' growled the policeman, making a fist. 'And an enemy who taunts us more with each manifestation. It's discouraging.'

'That said,' continued Owen, 'we do have some new information, some of it quite promising.'

So saying, he proceeded to report on our meeting with Wedekind, concerning Ziegler's children.

Still squinting at the upstairs window, the inspector lit a cigarette before replying:

'Interesting, very interesting, even though some of your assertions seem rather rash. The problem is, it will take a lot of time to verify.'

'Quite right,' agreed Owen, turning to look at him. 'But, with regard to Lethia, you must have some idea whether the Lethia you knew before is still the same.'

The policeman took several nervous puffs before replying:

'Yes, I think so... I'm almost certain it's the same person. But would I swear so under oath? That's a different matter.'

'You seem embarrassed, my dear fellow, if I'm not mistaken.'

'Well, yes... Because I haven't told you everything, neither you nor anyone else, for that matter.'

'About what?'

'About this,' he replied with a deep sigh, producing an envelope out of his pocket. He opened it and pulled out a black feather, saying:

'I found it here, at the foot of the wall, between tufts of grass. Because it's not an obvious clue, I kept it to myself. Perhaps you've already guessed, Mr. Burns?'

My friend looked hard at the inspector, then turned to me:

'What do you make of it, Achilles?'

After clearing my throat, I replied:

'Well, apart from the fact it's a feather from a large blackbird or a crow, I don't know what else to say... Wait a minute! It's from Miss Seagrave's tame crow!'

There was a pregnant silence. Then Lewis continued:

'Obviously it needs to be verified, but if it does turn out to be a crow's feather, that would be a supplementary charge against her. Although I have trouble understanding why she would encumber herself with a flying creature at such a time.'

'So do I,' agreed Owen. 'In fact, everything about the supposed route taken by the White Lady is strange, starting with her use of an open window. Sometimes she traverses walls and wire fences without difficulty, at other times she opens doors and windows in her path. And now, on the assumption it's Lethia, she needs to be accompanied by her pet crow... I don't know how you feel, but I have the impression of swimming in more and more troubled waters.'

The policeman sighed in agreement, then asked:

'Meanwhile, what should I do with this clue?'

'Consign it carefully, if possible, with other insignificant bits and pieces, under Objects Found. Nobody other than us will make the connection. You can always feign a sudden recollection, if need be. Meanwhile, we need to procure a feather from the suspect crow, in order to compare the two. Then we'll decide. But whatever the outcome, the presumptions against Miss Seagrave, however numerous, remain very slight from a judicial point of view. I haven't any advice to give you, inspector, other than to wait before sounding the charge.'

'Wait for what?'

'The results of Wedekind's searches. Because if one of the trails proves fruitful, that will have consequences. Meanwhile, it would be wise to have another meeting with Miss Seagrave, in order to collect a sample feather. Above all, you need to bring up old memories, in order to verify her identity. There must be something that an impostor could not know. And you're the only one who can do that.'

'Of course,' muttered the inspector. 'Consider it done!'

## 16

## A delicate mission

*October 30*

Ann closed her eyes, swallowed hard, and gave three discreet knocks on the door. Without waiting for a response she went into the study, where she found Vivian, as she expected.

Lady Richards, who had been leaning over the desk, straightened up:

'Yes, Ann, what can I do for you?'

'It's about the payment. Last month's wasn't transferred.'

'What payment?'

'You know very well. From Father.'

'You're talking about the cornucopia.'

'I beg your pardon?'

'Nothing my dear, nothing. It's noted. I'll discuss it with him later. It's his siesta now, as you well know.'

Ann bit her lip, trying hard not to scream. She detested these humiliating sessions, where she was reduced to feeling like a beggar outside a church, like the plague.

'Now I think about it,' continued Vivian, foraging amongst the papers on the desk. 'Where is it? ... Here it is. His last prescription from Dr. Sanders. Would you be a dear and pick it up from the pharmacy? I'm afraid I won't have time today.'

Then, looking at her stepdaughter, who hadn't budged an inch, she added, handing her the prescription:

'Ann, what's wrong? I'm not asking for the moon, after all. And it's for your father's sake... Oh! And if you have a second, please see Hildegard. She's prepared a shopping list... With all these events, we've fallen behind. Could you and Peter take care of it?'

'He's at work today.'

'Well then, ask John and Margot. Good grief, Ann, what is it with you today? It's as if I'm talking to that clumsy Janet!'

A few minutes later, Ann reached the salon and headed straight for the bar without even a glance at her sister, who had put her crossword down to watch her. She poured herself a glass of port, knocked it back in a single gulp, and poured herself another. Then she sat down next to her sister and burst into tears before getting what she had to say off her chest.

'Oh! My,' said Margot. 'I thought things were getting better between you two recently.'

'Yes,' said Ann, 'when we're dining or playing bridge. But when there's anything practical that needs to be done, she never misses an opportunity to humiliate me.'

'We're all a bit on edge these days, darling. When things have settled down, it will be better, you'll see.'

'It's been going on for quite a while,' retorted Ann, unconvinced. She rubbed her eyes. 'And you, Margot? I mean you and John. Do you regret coming here?'

'Not at all. But I don't think we'll stay forever. As soon as John has found work, we'll return to London.'

'Leaving us alone with that tigress?'

Margot winced and took her sister's hand.

'Three families under the same roof is too many in the long run. I think you and Peter should also consider leaving.'

'Then she would have succeeded in chasing us all out and her triumph would be complete.'

As her sister remained silent, Ann continued:

'And what does John think? He seems to have made a complete recovery. And how does he manage to stay so calm?'

'On the surface, maybe. But in his head, he must be pacing up and down like a lion in its cage. He's always been used to the open air and wide spaces, as you know. As far as his health is concerned, he has fully recovered, apart from occasional lapses of memory.'

'That's not obvious when he plays bridge. Nothing escapes him!'

'I'm not talking about that, darling, but of his memories that pre-date his tragic misadventures in Afghanistan. We've refrained from talking about it, but we know—.'

Just at that moment, the salon door opened.

'Well, talk of the devil,' said Margot with a smile.

John Peel's interruption was short-lived. He had only just joined the two young women when the doorbell rang. Telling them not to move, he left the salon.

'Inspector Lewis,' he said, greeting the visitor. 'I hope you're not the bearer of bad news?'

'No, I assure you. I merely came to make sure that your father-in-law's commitment to change the locks was carried out.'

'Yes. I took care of it myself and the work was finished yesterday. We can take a look together, if you wish?'

'I would be grateful. Thank you.'

Shortly afterwards, in front of the service door which opened onto the pantry leading to the kitchen, the major summarised:

'The locks on all the ground floor doors leading to the outside were changed, as well as some of the bolts. Also the few windows without wire grilles or mullions. At night we're locked down like a fortress now.'

'That's good, major, but it should have been done earlier.'

'Probably, but how were we to know? Everything was always so calm here.'

'I know,' sighed the inspector. 'Buckworth was never a hotbed of crime. A haven of peace, in fact, until that damned White Lady emerged from the limbo of our local legends.'

'How's your investigation going, by the way?'

'It's following its course,' replied Lewis prudently. 'But I'm not here full time, you know. I have to keep going back and forth to Oxford. There are a few leads—.'

'Do you want to talk about it over a drink?'

'Never whilst I'm on duty, thank you. And I'm also pressed for time. I still have to see one person.'

Moments later, the policeman was in his car, turning on the ignition. "The die is cast," he said to himself as the wheels crunched the gravel. Once in the village, he parked the vehicle near the inn and walked the rest of the way out of discretion—if that were possible in Buckworth. When he arrived in front of Lethia Seagrave's house, he frowned as he noticed that the pane of one of the windows had been replaced by a piece of cardboard. After taking a deep breath, he pressed the doorbell.

Half-an-hour later he felt better, albeit ashamed of his role. He realised his job required it sometimes, but he had found the double game he was obliged to play particularly painful. To create a climate of confidence, he had pushed hypocrisy as far as to stroke his hostess's furry friends, even though he had no affection for any of them. And he had quickly swallowed the refreshments she provided in order to increase the time he was alone to complete his mission: procuring a feather. Luckily, the crow was keeping them company on the veranda, and he had even thought about plucking one directly from the bird, which was not something they taught in police training college.

The rest of the mission had consisted of tests he had carefully prepared, two sets of questions pertaining to their memories of childhood. Real memories in the main, with one false in each set, all the better to trap his hostess. The first set had been a success, with Lethia reacting negatively to the single false one. When they got to the second set:

'... and that practical joke that went wrong, when young Tommy ended up in the nettles whilst he was running away. Do you remember?'

'Of course,' Lethia replied in amusement, but with her eyebrows betraying a certain perplexity.

'... and that same Tommy who fell into the slurry pit. It was a miracle that his uncle was there to pull him out by the hair.'

'I don't remember that at all. But it was all such a long time ago. Can I serve you some more lemonade?'

'Please, it's delicious.'

As the young woman left the room, he sighed with relief. He was now convinced that Lethia Seagrave was not an impostor. Now for the problem of the feather. He approached the crow, but as if by instinct, it started to flap its wings.

'Gently, gently. I'm not going to harm you.'

He tried again, with the same result. Then several times more, until he heard Lethia's voice behind his back.

'What exactly are you looking for, inspector?'

'Why, nothing. I was just....'

'Trying to pluck a feather? It would be simpler just to look behind the big blue pot. There should be one or two there.'

'But how...?'

'I didn't need my crystal ball. I simply heard the rumour.'

'Which rumour?'

'The one that says a feather from my crow was found near Sir Matthew's bedroom. Hadn't you heard it?'

'Yes and no... I hadn't heard the rumour, but it's a fact that we did find a feather.'

'Well then, help yourself. I've nothing to hide. But I can tell you that Iseult—that's her name—would never go there without me. And I haven't been to the manor recently, as I told you.'

As he sheepishly approached the pot, she continued:

'Do your job, inspector. I'd like to be cleared of suspicion as soon as possible. I don't find it amusing to get dirty looks whenever I stick my nose outside, or to see kids sticking their tongues out at me, when they're not breaking my windows. Didn't you notice the cardboard as you arrived?'

Yes, and it's very sad. If you know who did it, I'll take care of it.'

'The next time,' she said with a shrug of her shoulders. 'And as for the rest—I'm referring to that strange mish-mash of memories. I imagine that was done for a purpose? Did you have doubts about my identity?'

After having found and pocketed a feather, Lewis went over to his hostess:

'It's really not easy with you, Lethia. If all the witnesses I questioned were as quick-witted as you, I would have to change my profession. To answer your question, I can't discuss the case with you. At least for now. If you take my advice, I wouldn't stay here in the village much longer if I were you. You're young, you have talent, and you're not without resources. London seems like a better place for you.'

A gleam appeared in the young woman's dark eyes:

'Then who would look after my little companions?'

After leaving Lethia, Inspector Lewis headed for the inn. He sat at the bar, ordered a pint of ale, and struck up a conversation with the landlord. It was just after four o'clock and the place was almost empty. He spoke briefly about his visit to Lethia and asked if he'd heard talk about the discovery of the feather.

'Yes,' nodded Sam. 'I heard one or two of the lads talk about it.'

'When was that?'

'One or two days ago, I'd say.'

'Do you remember who they were?'

'No, sorry. You know, I hear so many things here. But between you and me, there's a lot of chatter about young Lethia.'

'I understand, Sam. Maybe I hadn't realised to what extent.'

'I know you're doing your best, but the sooner you solve this the better, Lewis. Feelings are running high.'

The policeman shrugged and ordered another beer.

'I say, Sam. Could I use your phone for a moment?'

In his cosy London flat, Owen Burns was re-reading a copy of Inspector Lewis's notes when the phone rang.

'Ah, it's you. I've been reading your remarks... Very instructive, my dear fellow. There are many small details which had escaped me...Have you any news?'

After listening to his correspondent, he declared:

'That's already a useful point, Lewis. So Lethia is not Deborah Ziegler.'

'That's right,' said the voice on the other end of the line. 'But the feather almost certainly comes from her pet crow. That needs to be verified by an expert, but to the naked eye there's no doubt. But that raises another problem. Are you sure neither you nor your friend Mr. Stock breathed a word about our discovery to anyone?'

'Absolutely. Why?'

After listening to the policeman's story, Owen said pensively:

'Very strange, that leak. It could signify two things... but let me think about it. Getting back to your notes—and I must congratulate you on your conscientious work—I noted two items which leave me perplexed. First, there's Sir Matthew's bedside book which seems to have been mislaid. I wasn't aware of that. The second point is to do with the chronological sequence of events. Your notes highlight a crucial point which, in fact... changes everything. It's too delicate a matter to discuss over the phone, but we'll talk about it later. Meanwhile, keep your eyes open and don't hesitate to contact me if need be.'

## 17

### Where has Sir Matthew gone?

*November 5*

The last rays of the sun had just disappeared over the horizon. Night fell on Buckworth and the air freshened. In the vast salon of Buckworth House, a cheerful fire was crackling in the hearth. The clock was chiming six o'clock as Sir Matthew got up from his armchair and said to his wife:

'I'm going to get some fresh air, darling. I'm leaving my daughters in your capable hands.'

Vivian agreed with an amiable smile which vanished as soon as the door closed behind her husband.

'As regular as a Swiss watch,' commented Major John Peel, getting up in turn.

'He's been like that for a while,' replied Vivian. 'I think that, in addition to his medicaments, Dr. Sanders prescribed a regular daily routine: breakfast, first walk, lunch, siesta, second walk... You're right, John. It's like living with a programmed robot.'

'Do you blame him?' asked Ann sharply. 'If you want your "robot" to keep functioning, I advise you....'

'What you mean is that previously he did whatever he wanted.'

'Right,' said John, after clearing his throat. 'I'm going to unwind with a game of billiards. Peter's waiting for me.'

'Wish him good luck from me,' said Margot mockingly. 'And don't stay too long.'

After the major had left the room, Margot continued:

'Why do we spend our time waiting for men?'

'That's a good question,' replied Vivian. 'Maybe it won't be long before women seize power! Has there ever been a society run by women?'

'Yes, the Amazons,' replied Ann.

'Mmm,' reflected Margot. 'Didn't they cut off one breast so they could fire their arrows better?'

'It was an exclusively feminine society,' added Ann.

'Then how did they reproduce?'

'Quite simply, they went on raids to rape males.'

'Ah, well, we can but dream,' said Vivian laughingly.

The conversation continued in the same vein until Esther appeared a quarter-of-an-hour later, at which point Ann left to change her blouse, which she had stained with port earlier.

Shortly thereafter, in the billiard room, Peter sighed in exasperation after having missed an easy shot.

'I've had a bad start and I don't think it's going to get any better. Do you feel like a drink?'

'Already? We've only just started.'

'I insist, old boy. Unless you want to grind me into the dust.'

'Very well,' sighed John. 'If you don't mind listening to chatterboxes.'

As they returned to the salon, just after Ann, the clock struck half-past six.

'That's odd,' said Vivian, her eyes on the clock. 'Matthew isn't back yet. Normally he goes out for twenty minutes at the most.'

After serving Peter and himself a drink, John remarked:

'We're not going to time his sorties with a stop-watch, are we? Unless that was also in the doctor's prescription.'

'Maybe,' said Peter. 'Unless it's the gospel according to St. Vivian!'

The two men burst into laughter.

Vivian went pale and her eyes flashed in anger.

'You're as bad as each other. You're horrible, both of you.'

'Be serious, my dear,' replied John. 'You're not going to worry about such a small thing, surely?'

'Have you forgotten Matthew's condition?'

'Of course not, but he's only been gone ten minutes more—.'

'Nearly fifteen, now,' replied Vivian with another anxious look at the clock. 'I'm telling you, it's not normal.'

Peter had just served himself another drink, which he had swallowed as quickly as the first. Approaching Vivian, he said curtly:

'Let's be serious for a moment. You don't expect us to believe you're really concerned for your husband, do you?'

Standing up to face him, and looking him straight in the eye, the young Lady Richards replied coldly but calmly:

'Yes, I'm concerned. And I'm asking you to calm down.'

Disconcerted, Peter turned scarlet. Then he sniggered to no one in particular:

'What's all this nonsense? Everyone here knows she's only waiting for one thing: the old man kicking the bucket!'

A sepulchral silence followed the outburst. Then Peter continued heatedly:

'Nobody says anything? Nobody has the courage to look things in the face, for once?'

It was as if he were surrounded by statues. He turned to John for support, but in vain. The major didn't react. Red with rage and confusion, Peter left the salon, slamming the door behind him.

Several seconds elapsed in deathly silence, then Vivian broke down in tears. Ann placed a hand on her arm.

'Please excuse him, my dear. I don't know what came over him.'

'Yes, it was inadmissible,' added Margot. 'Don't you agree, John?'

'Absolutely,' agreed the major. 'We're all on edge, and have been for some time. Obviously, he didn't mean it.'

'Be quiet,' sobbed Vivian. 'I don't believe you.'

'For heaven's sake,' said Ann. 'We're not monsters, you know.'

Esther tried to calm Vivian, without success. It was several minutes before the young woman stopped crying, but her anger remained. Looking at the clock, which showed a quarter to seven, she exclaimed:

'He's still not here!'

She broke free from the protective arms of Esther and Margot and stood up:

'You can stay here if you like. I know what I have to do....'

Her red dress swished behind her as she headed for the door, which slammed violently behind her. They could hear her footsteps crossing the hall. Then the sound of the front door slamming.

Another deathly silence. Everyone looked at each other, then John announced:

'I'm going after her. With what she has on her back, she won't be very warm.'

'It is strange, all the same,' said Ann. 'She's probably right, now I think about it. Father should have been back some time ago.'

Margot and Esther looked at each other and agreed to follow John. But before they all had a chance to leave, new footsteps echoed in the hall and the salon door was flung wide open. It was Vivian, even paler than before.

'I saw her,' she stammered, a wild look in her eye. 'She's there, outside.'

'Who the devil are you talking about?' asked the major sharply.

'The White Lady... She crossed the driveway... only a few seconds... But it was her, I'm quite sure!'

A few moments later they were inspecting the illuminated area around the manor. Meanwhile, Peter, alerted by the noises, had joined them. Then, armed with flashlights, they ventured farther down the driveway to a point several yards from the wire fence, where Vivian affirmed she had seen the White Lady. Their search did not last long. A few minutes later, the beam from the major's flashlight alighted on the inert body of Sir Matthew, lying at the foot of a tree. After a rapid examination, John turned to his companions and shook his head solemnly. But before the beam moved away, they were all able to see the face of the deceased, frozen in an unspeakable expression of fright.

## 18

### The missing book

*November 6*

'Well, our White Lady finally got what she wanted,' sighed Inspector Lewis, his head down, his fingers drumming the table. 'She's won all along the line.'

That afternoon, in the almost deserted bar of the inn, the policeman reported the principle elements of the investigation to Owen, who had just arrived from London, having been alerted to the latest tragedy.

'We shan't have the autopsy report until tomorrow,' he continued, 'but the examiner doesn't think it will differ much from his original diagnosis: Sir Matthew died following a violent emotional shock, probably due to intense fear. And having seen the corpse, with its eyes popping out of its head and its contracted jaw, I can only agree. Particularly since there was not a single suspicious mark on the body, such as a bump, a bruise, or a scratch.'

Owen nodded pensively.

'The last view of this world, for Sir Matthew, would probably have been the sweet smile of Death, or her white fingers seeking him out... He was certainly well prepared for it, given the numerous appearances of our White Lady.'

'And an easy prey for her.'

'Do you think that just the sight of her, as he was walking in the park would have been enough to strike him down?'

'It appears not. I asked that question of the examiner, who said it was highly unlikely.'

'So she engaged in some secret manoeuvre. But what? What could have frightened Sir Matthew to that extent? Let me see, you said that the body was found at the foot of a tree, not far from the wire fence?'

'Yes, at least ten yards from the gravel driveway and about the same from the wire fence. And a good fifty yards from the entrance to the manor, which more or less eliminates his spouse from the list of suspects. Between the time she left the building and her return, when she announced that she'd seen the White Lady, less than a minute had elapsed, according to all the witnesses. Difficult for her, under those conditions, to have executed any kind of plan. As for the others, no one has a solid alibi. During Sir Matthew's absence, each was away for at least ten minutes, with one exception: Margot Peel, who never left the salon for a single moment.'

A smile appeared on Owen's face.

'Hmm. You say that as if you think she's guilty.'

'No, I'm merely noting the facts. I've prepared a summary of everyone's movements between the hours of six and seven o'clock, spanning the period between the last time he was seen alive and the discovery of his body, which also corresponds to the time of death according to the medical examiner.'

He pulled a sheet of paper from his pocket and placed it on the table.

'You can keep it, Mr. Burns. I have a copy.'

'That's very helpful, thank you. I imagine you've also combed the area around the tree and found nothing, otherwise you would have told me.'

'Correct. Nothing in particular. In any case, no crow's feather this time,' he added jokingly. 'Ah! Did I tell you? The two feathers are identical, according to the police laboratory. The feather beneath Sir Matthew's window did indeed come from Miss Seagrave's crow.'

The policeman finished his beer, stroked his moustache with the back of his hand, and smiled.

'And, speaking of Miss Seagrave, things are starting to get interesting.'

'You've questioned her? I assume she still has no alibi?'

'One thing at at time, Mr. Burns. Yes, I questioned her, just before lunch in fact, and I'm happy to announce that this time she may have an alibi.'

'Well done!'

'I stress "may",' added Lewis mischievously. 'Because there's very tight timing involved and I still have to question witnesses. Plus which....'

He bent down to reach the leather bag at his feet, from which he pulled out a brown paper envelope which he opened. He extracted a piece of paper folded in four.

'You can read it yourself. It's the message which Miss Seagrave claims to have found in her letter box yesterday morning. In capital letters, with no signature, as you can see.'

'Bizarre,' said Owen, after having examined it.

'To say the least. But I think it's best to confirm her alibi before drawing conclusions.'

'I leave that up to you.'

'And that's not all,' continued Lewis. 'I spoke to the Richards family solicitor on the phone. I know him personally and he had no problem sketching out the deceased's last wishes. You may be in for a surprise.'

'What kind of surprise?'

'One small and one very big. For the first, we'll wait a little. But for the second....'

He looked right and left and leant towards my friend.

'I don't think the walls here have ears, but you never know.'

'You're pulling my leg, Inspector. We're the only ones in the room.'

'Listen.'

After the inspector had whispered a few words in his ear, Owen nodded his head and smiled.

'I actually expected it. But it was only a hypothesis. But there's likely to be quite a commotion when the will is officially read out!'

'It's planned for the day after tomorrow. I'll keep you informed. Last but not least....'

The policeman reached into his bag again and produced an envelope bigger and thicker than the first.

'Another surprise?' exclaimed Owen in delight. 'Decidedly, that's quite a bag of tricks!'

'It's partly due to you, in fact. Do you remember a previous phone call where you enquired about a missing book?'

'Sir Matthew's bedside book.'

'Yes. Well, here it is.'

As he pulled it gingerly out of the envelope, Owen asked:

'How did you find it?'

'After you mentioned it, I enquired at the mansion about it during one of my visits, but I only received it this morning. It was Lady

Richards who found it in the small study, amongst a stack of other documents. She would not have noticed it but for the peculiar cover.'

Smiling broadly, Owen contemplated the object in his hands. With its moiré effect in black and violet, the cover resembled a briefcase. He opened it and found a number of elegantly handwritten pages, nearly thirty in all, on thick paper.

'I don't know her handwriting, but I'm willing to bet it's Miss Seagrave's. And this is the prose written whilst she was in a trance—what she called automatic writing. Have you read them?'

'I just took a quick look at the first, which seemed surreal. But I imagine you'll be able to make some pertinent deductions.'

'Yes, and I've just done so,' replied Owen, leafing through the pages. 'I can assure you this is a major step forward in the affair, and the days of our White Lady are henceforth numbered!'

There was a silence, then Lewis asked:

'What do you plan to do now?'

'First of all, I would like to see Miss Seagrave again.'

'You're out of luck. She's in London right now. She told me she had a number of appointments in her office.'

Owen consulted his fob watch.

'Three-thirty,' he said. 'If I catch the next train, I can be there by late afternoon. I'm sure she'll be gracious enough to grant me a session after the other clients have gone.'

Then, placing his hand on the moiré cover, he asked suddenly:

'May I borrow this? It will give me something to read on the train.'

# 19

## Clairvoyance session

A heavy silence hung over the room. Thick velvet curtains, alternating between deep violet and emerald green, formed the backdrop. Lighted candles in two candelabra provided the lighting, in which several pieces of crystal-ware sparkled. Here and there, cabalistic signs decorated the backs of gilded books and chests of precious wood. But on the small round table in the centre of the room, there was only a black velvet table-cloth on which Lethia's fingers were spread as she looked at her visitor with an impenetrable stare. With her violet turban, her vaguely Eurasian looks, and her eyes that shone like black diamonds, she could have passed for a pagoda goddess. Her gold earrings and the strands of gold and silver in her turban gave her a mystical allure.

Despite being familiar with paranormal séances, Owen was impressed. Ten minutes earlier he had been in the bustling and noisy Oxford Street and had stopped in front of the entrance, not imagining that his surroundings were about to change dramatically, despite the plaque, which announced, in gilt letters: *"Lethia, Daughter of the River of Forgetfulness, Clairvoyant."* The full extent of the change only struck him after he went though the door. He was in luck, for Lethia had just received her last client and was about to close shop.

'Why didn't you say anything?' he asked, after a long silence.

The young woman smiled faintly.

'Did you come for a consultation or for an investigation, Mr. Burns?'

'Both. Because, for me, you can't have one without the other. So I repeat my question: why the silence?'

'What are you talking about?'

'You know very well. Unless you've lost all your powers.'

With a shrug of her shoulders she gave in.

'Because I'd promised. It was a secret between us, and was to remain so until his death.'

'I confess to having become suspicious when you talked about your studies. You hesitated when you spoke of funds, and I told myself that your mother would not have been able to afford them. So I asked myself who....'

'Is it really important right now, Mr. Burns?'

'Yes, as far as the investigation is concerned. Speaking of which, I must tell you that there's no point in trying to find one of your attempts at automatic writing for us to examine.'

'Aren't you interested any more?'

'Yes, more than ever! But I now have everything to hand. Here, let me show you.'

So saying, he produced the book he had borrowed from Inspector Lewis.

The young woman, amused, leafed through it. Owen continued:

'It's your handwriting, is that not so?'

'Naturally. And I recognise the cover.'

'How did it get into Sir Matthew's hands?'

'He came to my house for a card reading. Like you, he was intrigued by my "writings" and he asked to borrow it.'

'And you didn't tell us?'

'No. Why should I? It wasn't the first time he'd borrowed something from me.'

'I assume you've read it?'

'No, actually. I prefer a little retrospection in such cases. How to put it? Sometimes distance allows a better comprehension of the message. And since I'd written it the day before, or the day before that....'

'So you haven't read the text?' insisted Owen.

'No, I'm afraid not. I thought about it afterwards, but after all that happened, it was difficult. And Sir Matthew hadn't paid me another visit. Nevertheless, I learnt that the book had got mislaid. Someone told me, but I can't remember who.'

'Perhaps Peter Corsham, who also visited you for a consultation?'

'You're right. It must have been him. He's the only member of the Richards clan I've seen since.'

'I find it hard to believe you, Miss Seagrave.'

'Nevertheless, that's what happened.'

'I'm talking about your claim not to know the fruits of your automatic writing.'

'Is it that important?'

'You wouldn't ask if you had read it.'

'So,' she said ironically. 'I'd better correct my oversight right away. But I warn you, that might take some time.'

'No,' retorted Owen, taking the book back. 'We'll talk about it at the appropriate time.'

Preoccupied by what he had just learnt, Owen found it hard to concentrate when Lethia suggested he select three cards.

'You seem tense, Mr. Burns, so let's just limit ourselves to one single card. If I'd talked about the past, you would have accused me of trickery, because you're a public figure and much is known about you. Likewise, as to the present, one can easily imagine the problems facing you. That leaves the future. May I remind you that yours is now the hand of destiny. Try to concentrate....'

After some hesitation, Owen picked a card out of the pack that Lethia had spread out in front of him. She turned it over. It was a crude circle, drawn in chalk on a rock face.

'The circle,' murmured Lethia. 'It's one of the best signs, if not the best.'

'And... what does it mean?'

'Many things, but essentially the circle of life, the rebirth, the infinite cycle of the gravitation of the stars, the galaxies, and even the universe. At the risk of being excessive, it could mean you are eternal. No one is, of course. In your case, I believe it corresponds to great fame, which will endure even after you leave this earth.'

'Hmm... I don't know that I believe you, but it's still a pleasure to hear it.'

'In any case, it seems to have given you confidence. That will enable you to go farther. Have you a precise question?'

'Yes, and you know what it is. What I would like to know is who is hiding behind the mask of the White Lady?'

With an enigmatic smile Lethia stared hard at him:

'I believe you already have an idea.'

'Maybe,' replied Owen, just as enigmatically. 'But a proof or a clue would be welcome.'

A few moments later, the detective had chosen three new cards, aligned face down on the black velvet, forming a mystical barrier between himself and the clairvoyant. Despite all logic, he sensed that the moment was crucial.

'Just to be clear, Mr. Burns,' declared Lethia solemnly. 'Don't expect conclusive evidence. They will simply be significant elements to guide you. After you leave here, the images will follow you and, whether you like it or not, consciously or not, will steer your investigation. Do you still want to continue?'

'More than ever.'

'Well then, let's start. Turn over the card of your choice.'

With a shaking hand, Owen revealed a picture of an Indian tepee in isolation on a great plain.

'Hmm...,' said Lethia thoughtfully. 'It symbolises the home, a refuge, an intimate place, which might need adapting to present times. So I would say a cabin, a house, a hotel, a building of some sort. Let's look at the next one.'

The next card revealed a heart painted a flamboyant red.

'Love, passion, of course,' observed Lethia. 'But note that the card is the wrong way up. Which means the the symbolism must also be taken the other way. Hate, jealousy, perhaps clandestine affairs. I would add that, at this stage, it would be wise to establish a connection between the two cards, which only you can do.'

The third card showed a flock of birds in a luminous sky.

'Lots of feathers!' exclaimed Lethia. 'Swallows, ravens, it's hard to tell.'

'Or crows,' joked Owen. 'You can't avoid them!'

'For my part, the message is less clear than the previous two. I would be careful of associating it with them. Particularly since we are influenced by what you have evoked. Nonetheless, you mustn't lose sight of it. There's a reason it's there. I can't tell you more than that.'

His eyes glued to the three cards, Owen declared in an emotional voice:

'My hand has just been strengthened by three trump cards.'

'Undoubtedly. But it's up to you to make good use of them.'

## 20

## A bird's name

*November 7*

London was bathed in sunlight. Its rays seemed to encourage the feverish human activity, giving it energy and good humour. But that was not the case for Superintendent Frank Wedekind, even though he enjoyed a beautiful view of the sun-filled capital from his office window at Scotland Yard. The source of his irritation was the large block of cast iron just below the window.

'Damned radiator!' he groused, manhandling the control switch. 'It has a mind of its own. It heats when it's not supposed to, or emits a Siberian cold when it's fully open. It's been going on for two weeks now.'

Owen Burns, seated at his friend's desk, asked:

'Haven't you contacted maintenance?'

'Of course! There have been dozens of them, all with the same refrain. "There, that should do it. Don't hesitate to call if there's still a problem." A bunch of incompetents, all of them. I'd better open the window wide if we don't want to end up being boiled alive.'

After wiping his brow with the back of his hand, he sat down facing the detective and sighed:

'I can't wait for retirement.'

'It won't be tomorrow, by the looks of it.'

'No, but I'm thinking about it more and more.'

'What will you do? Have you thought about it?'

'I know what I'm not going to do, Burns. No more chasing anarchists, Bolsheviks, crooks, evildoers, thieves and thugs of all stripes. I've given my best and risked my life, and I've concluded it was all to no purpose. You put five in jail and the judges release ten. You'd think there was a link between the high-ups and the parasites. And we poor fools take it in the neck from everyone.'

'Come now, Wedekind. You're painting too black a picture. There must have been a few artful murderers who've given you professional satisfaction.'

'Yes, but those are the cases *you* bring. We plebs have the mundane daily routine I complained about.'

'So let's talk about the case in hand.'

'Very well. Who goes first? You have some news, I understand.'

Owen summarised the situation, notably his most recent discoveries, then added:

'And this morning, I even had some news from Lewis.'

'He's a good lad, that one, what do you think?' asked Wedekind, lighting a cigarette.

'There's no doubt about it. He's conscientious, energetic, thoughtful and diplomatic when need be. I'm thinking of the crow's feather, temporarily "mislaid". That finally prodded the culprit into committing an error... And this morning, he filled me in on the autopsy report he'd just received.'

'Ah?' exclaimed Wedekind with a gleam in his eye. 'The old man didn't die of a heart attack after all?'

'Yes, everything is according to the initial diagnosis. But there's a detail, a tiny detail, which is food for thought.'

'What?'

'Something was found in the hair which is difficult to explain in the normal manner of things. Tiny, as I said, but there's no doubt about it: on the hair, at the level of the left parietal bone, they found traces of burnt powder.'

'Caused by an explosion? Or a shot?'

'Apparently so. But from afar or very attenuated, so much so that we can't work out the origin. Lewis is going to go over the area again, but I doubt that will yield much in an outdoor environment.'

'You're probably right. But it does suggest new avenues to explore. I'm thinking about an explosion or an intense light, triggered at a distance through some ingenious artifice.'

'A blinding light which fatally blinded Sir Matthew? It's hard to imagine. The theory of an explosion or a shot is more credible. The problem is that no one at the mansion heard any detonation.'

'Which you seem to regret.'

'Perhaps,' said Owen thoughtfully. 'It makes me think of... never mind. What do you have to report?'

Wedekind picked up a file from his desk and leafed through it.

'No bombshells, but still... Regarding the Ziegler case, things have evolved faster than I expected. In most cases, we were able to clear things up by a simple process of elimination. We're now certain that none of the persons incriminated could be the vengeful daughter or son, with two exceptions. For the first, because it's practically unverifiable. For the second, anything is possible if we envisage what I will call a double substitution. In other words, a very far-fetched solution. If that were the case, the Yard probably could not be of any help. Only someone close or intimate could unmask the impostor. Do you get my meaning?'

'Perfectly. But to move the investigation in that direction would be to tip our hand.'

'Otherwise, there's still the possibility of someone outside the group. Someone from the village, for example.'

Owen looked pensive.

'I've already thought about that. But you would have to know everyone in that little world. I'll talk to Lewis. He's by far the most qualified for the task. That said, I'm happy you've concluded your investigation of the Ziegler children. A brilliantly conducted investigation, as usual, and I congratulate you. All the better because I have another small favour to ask.'

With a knowing smile, the superintendent sat upright and crossed his fingers.

'I knew you wouldn't be paying me flowery compliments without a reason. I'm listening.'

'Before that, I'd like to share my thoughts with you, which have become more refined since the discovery—or, rather, reappearance—of Sir Matthew's bedside book, Lethia's famous notes that I've told you about.'

For the next fifteen minutes, the detective spoke without interruption, to the accompaniment of approving nods.

'Well,' said Wedekind at the end. 'It's becoming clearer. In fact, I would say you've made gigantic steps. What an incredible business, although obvious once you know.'

'The problem is that I have no proof so far.'

'And is that where I come in?'

'Yes. Yesterday I had a sort of intuition.'

'An intuition? Quite a departure from your usual methods.'

'Let's just say I'm channelling my thoughts in support of a vision which came to me as the result of... never mind what. I told myself that we would have to find the proof in the past.'

'An investigation in the past, that sounds promising.'

'The recent past, let me hasten to add, which I believe to be just a few months before the principal events. Here's my idea....'

Once again, Wedekind listened to his friend in silence for a few moments, then exclaimed:

'What? That's what you call a small service? You might just as well look for a needle in a haystack!'

'There is some similarity, I agree.'

'I don't doubt it. But those are not real names, and we would need photos for identification. Do you have any other clues?'

'Possibly. The establishment may be named after a bird.'

'Like *The Eagle? The Three Doves? The Cuckoo's Nest*?'

'For example, yes. It's only a supposition. Maybe it's best to forget about it. It's too vague and it might be a waste of time.'

'I need to know what you want, Burns. Have you any idea how many hotels and pubs there are in the capital?'

'You might limit yourself to the principal axis, between the presumed point of departure and arrival.'

'Even so, I haven't got enough men at my disposal for that.'

'And yet I feel sure there must be proof somewhere. And I've thought of something. Very chancy, I admit, but it could save a lot of time. Normally payments in such cases are made in cash, out of discretion. But it's possible, occasionally, for it to be done by cheque, if for some reason there's not enough cash. Checking bank accounts for that period could be instructive. That would limit your search to a small number of establishments. It would obviously require a huge stroke of luck.'

'I prefer that, Burns. We can get that done in forty-eight hours. I'll get on to it. By the way, what happened to Mr. Stock, the big fellow, your faithful lieutenant? Is he avoiding you?'

'No. Unfortunately, he's busy. But he's reserved a seat for the final denouement.'

'Imminent, from what I gather?'

'Yes. If you bring me the proof I need.'

## 21

### The will

*November 8*

There was a deathly silence the following afternoon in the salon of Buckworth Manor. When the clock struck three o'clock it was like a death knell. All the household was present, including the entire family. Lethia Seagrave was also present, as well as Owen Burns and Inspector Lewis, who seemed to be mounting guard at her side. Very few people looked at her, but when they did it was always with disdain. The purpose of the meeting was twofold: clarifications on the case of the White Lady, and the reading of the will by the solicitor, who was keeping everyone waiting.

Shortly afterwards, the sound of a car could be heard, accompanied by the crunch of tyres on the gravel. When the lawyer appeared, he excused himself for his tardiness, with a glibness that was anything but sincere. He was a small man with a wrinkled face and a double chin. Out of habit, or to draw attention to himself, he cleared his throat prior to each utterance.

'Hmm... Very well,' he said, sitting down at the large table and opening his briefcase, 'First of all, I need to make it clear that it has not yet been possible to establish a precise evaluation of the deceased's estate. Between two-thirds and three-quarters are stocks, treasury bonds and other instruments, whose value is yet to be determined. Also gold ingots and jewellery in various vaults to which we have not yet gained access. I would guess their sum at two or three times the value of this property. Sir Matthew, may his soul be at rest, simplified matters by dividing his estate into shares, after deducting one-tenth to go to certain charitable works, but the bulk to Miss Esther Adey, here present, for her "loyal service and friendship, so precious to me over my long existence".'

Tears came into the housekeeper's eyes and she nodded her head, as much in approval as posthumous recognition.

For the next ten minutes, the solicitor read out a long list of charitable works, to signs of growing impatience from those present.

'As for the rest,' he concluded, 'it's much more simple. Sir Matthew left half of his remaining fortune to Lady Vivian Richards, née Marsh, and the other half to be divided in equal parts amongst his children.'

'Is that all?' cut in Ann.

'Er, yes.'

'Bravo!' she exclaimed, clapping her hands. 'You've won, Vivian, it's a masterstroke! The least one can say is that your marriage of a few weeks really paid off.'

'Please, Ann,' replied the lady of the manor. 'A little decency, if you please. I'm sure Matthew would disapprove if he were still amongst us.'

'Aren't you going to say anything, Peter?' continued Ann furiously. 'What about you, Margot, or you, John?'

Then a strange smile appeared on her lips as she looked at Lethia.

'Well, at least there's someone else who's equally disappointed. Someone who may have paid as much as our young widow with her body, but without getting anything in exchange. It's a real pity that father forgot your little attentions and failed to mention you in his will.'

'I fear there's a slight misunderstanding,' said the solicitor after clearing his throat.

'In what way?' replied Ann, offended.

'Miss Seagrave is indeed mentioned.'

'But didn't you just say....'

'... that the other half would be divided between the children? Yes, but there are three. You, Margot... and Lethia Seagrave.'

There was a moment of stupor, whilst all eyes went from the lawyer to Lethia. Then Ann broke the silence with a hysterical shriek:

'And you never said anything?'

The clairvoyant shook her head:

'No. My father expressly asked me not to. For reasons you will readily understand, he wanted his relationship with my mother to remain a secret, as well as the fruit of their passion, so to speak.'

'And you allowed us to think....'

'I didn't allow you to think anything at all. And I might add that if anyone was left out, it was I, who was deprived of the golden childhood that you enjoyed.'

After a moment's hesitation, Ann continued:

'You won't get away with it! We'll get the will annulled.'

'I very much doubt that, madam,' said the lawyer. 'The will was drawn up in my presence, in full accordance with the law, and I can certify that the late Sir Matthew was of sound mind and body at the time. Having said that, and with your permission, I will leave you now. We will have the opportunity to meet again once there is more information.' Gathering his papers, he added: 'I was forgetting. There's a letter from your father to you, Miss Seagrave.'

So saying, he handed her a brown envelope.

There was still a general stupor in the room as the lawyer left. That was when Owen Burns began to speak:

'I imagine it will take several days for some of you to become accustomed to the new situation, but the mystery of the White Lady remains, with its host of shadows, some of which I shall attempt to dissipate.'

'But don't we already know who it is?' screeched Ann. 'It's that devilish creature who did everything to grab her share of the cake in the shortest possible time!'

'It can only be her, it's obvious,' added Peter, siding with his wife. 'This will is all the proof you need.'

'Your suspicions appear to have merit at first sight,' said Owen in a soothing voice. 'But let's take a closer look, starting with one of the principal puzzles of the affair, namely the disappearance of the White Lady from the small studio with the deceased hot on her heels about a month and a half ago. It appeared to be an inexplicable feat, but the recent discovery of Sir Matthew's "bedside book", thanks to Lady Richards, proved decisive. This "bedside book" is in fact what one might call a short story, written by Miss Seagrave. It's an informal text, more or less inspired, but very revealing. I shall summarise it in a few words. It's about Death, its mystery, its incarnation in the form of a white lady, and the specific history of our local White Lady. Her beautiful face, her terrifying white hands and the cold she emits are all described with an undeniable evocative talent. The text, according to Miss Seagrave, was written during a sort of trance, as is her custom, and was not destined for any particular reader, like any other similar texts. But one day her father borrows it from her....

'What's clear in all this is that, if we'd had that information, if we'd known that Sir Matthew had read it before going to sleep that night, we would immediately have realised that he had relived the story in the form of a nightmare a few hours later. A nightmare so terrifying and so distressing that he sincerely believed it to be true. Remember he was the only one to have seen, or believe he had seen, the White Lady that night. All the others had merely followed him to the small studio where he shut himself in to—as he believed—trap the White Lady, who had only existed in his imagination. And if he'd had any doubts afterwards, he'd committed himself too much to be able to retract. Out of fear of being treated like an old madman, he may even have sought to convince himself by embellishing his tale with details of the ghost's face and general appearance. To cap it all, the fact that Ann and Peter had seen her three months earlier must have reinforced his conviction. To summarise, the explanation of that puzzle was a simple nightmare, but it was the starting point for what was to follow.'

'Well then,' exclaimed Ann, 'it's even clearer! Knowing all that, Miss Seagrave simply followed through with a series of tangible interventions until father eventually died of fear.'

'That would undoubtedly be one's first reaction. But there's a problem. Miss Seagrave swears she's never read the text.'

'*And you believe her?*' shrieked Ann, almost choking.

'Whether I believe her or not, it's a fact that anyone could have read the book, which mysteriously disappeared for several weeks.'

'One would think you're taking sides, Mr. Burns,' hissed Ann vehemently.

'And I must say I think so too,' added Vivian.

'Not at all,' replied Owen calmly. 'And you'll soon understand why. Because what followed made it obvious that someone was manoeuvring to place the blame on Miss Seagrave. We had found a crow's feather under Sir Matthew's bedroom window, apparently very compromising for her. Inspector Lewis and I scrupulously guarded the information, but a few days later people were talking about it in the village. So I ask you: who other than the real culprit, wishing to implicate Miss Seagrave and frustrated by our silence, could have spread the rumour?

'And that's not all. Last Tuesday—the day of Sir Matthew's death—Miss Seagrave found an anonymous message in her letter box. It said, "If you want information about the author of the feather be outside the manor tonight at 7 p.m. precisely". I'm assuming "author of the feather" refers to whomever placed it under Sir Matthew's window to compromise her. Which in itself shows she's not guilty.'

'That's completely ridiculous!' exclaimed Vivian. 'She wrote the message herself, clearly.'

'It's blindingly obvious,' agreed Ann.

'Let us continue,' said Owen imperturbably. 'Miss Seagrave, who is far from naïve, senses a trap. She goes to the rendezvous, but more than an hour early. It's a quarter to six and it's already dark. She spies a furtive shadow in the park, which she unfortunately does not recognise. But she instinctively senses a plot and beats a retreat.'

After another silence, Ann returned to the attack.

'I'm beginning to think, Mr. Burns, that your reputation is undeserved.'

'And why, may I ask?'

Sarcastically, she raised her arms in the air.

'And he says it so innocently!' Her eyes blazing with anger, she spat out the words. *'Because you believe whatever she tells you!'*

'Not only I, my dear madam, Inspector Lewis as well. He recently took down the testimony of the Nicholls family, here in the village, whom you undoubtedly know. Patrick Nicholls, his wife, her parents and their three children all swear that Miss Seagrave visited them that night at a quarter to six and stayed there for two hours without a break. It is therefore proved beyond doubt that Miss Seagrave, your half-sister let me remind you, could not have killed your father that night because he was still alive at six o'clock. We must therefore seek the murderer elsewhere.'

## 22

### Sir Matthew's grave

*November 10*

As the first shovelfuls of earth fell on the coffin, Lethia could not contain her tears. She had managed to cope during the eulogy, even though she had felt that the portrait he had painted of her father was excessive in many regards. And she and her late mother were certainly in a position to know. But there was something tragically definitive about the burial. Her sole link with the village, and indeed elsewhere, had just been severed. And, although her father wasn't perfect, he loved her much more than she knew. His posthumous letter to her had made that abundantly clear, with its simple but profoundly moving words.

As the coffin disappeared, she thought she saw his face... She stiffened and turned around. She was alone now, all alone, and surrounded by those hostile to her.

Would she make up with Margot one day? It wasn't out of the question. Lethia had detected signs of emotion behind that impassive exterior when she had learnt that they were half-sisters. But the same could not be said of Ann, with whom the hostilities were likely to be permanent. And the same was true of Vivian, although that didn't bother her one little bit. The furious look from those black panther eyes had no effect. Similarly with Peter. Since the reading of the will he had regarded her with nothing but contempt. Esther had remained as impassive as ever, but she had at least expressed her condolences, as had John Peel, who had given her a compassionate smile. He was a decent sort, who had also had a hard life, yet had never said a harsh word about her or looked askance. Inspector Lewis had also greeted her. She had not forgotten his duplicity during questioning as he attempted to collect the crow's feather, but he was only doing his job, she supposed. And at present he seemed relieved that she had been cleared of all suspicion. Despite their age difference, she considered him to be an old friend, at least previously. And maybe again.

She looked discreetly around the gathering, which was beginning to disperse. She hadn't seen Owen Burns. Although his presence wasn't obligatory, she felt mildly disappointed. In fact, she didn't really know how she felt about him. Sometimes he annoyed her with his caustic irony—even though she gave as good as she got—but at other times he displayed surprising sensitivity. She smiled to herself and shrugged her shoulders.

Treading on the wet grass of the cemetery, she crossed diagonally in the direction of her house, where she was warmly greeted by her little companions, each in its own way. Enthusiastically by her dog—an old beagle with doleful eyes—very demonstrative as usual; more languidly by her three cats, who curled up by her ankles; and discreetly by her rabbit. As for the crow, it emitted its usual double caw. After stoking the fire in the hearth, she threw herself into her armchair, suddenly very weary. Her father's letter lay on the side table. She had re-read it several times, and each time had thought about throwing it in the fire, so as to finally break with the past, with its painful memories. She picked it up once again, and tears came to her eyes as she read it. But this time she crumpled it up and threw it in the fire, after which she curled up, convulsed with sobs.

Owen Burns was in his London apartment, in front of the fire, assiduously reading a treatise on criminology. Beside him on the carpet was a stack of similar tomes, which he had searched in vain. Leafing through the pages, he grumbled aloud to himself. He was sure the article he was looking for was there somewhere.

The sound of the telephone froze him to the spot, but he recovered quickly.

'Wedekind,' he said after a moment's hesitation. 'What a pleasant surprise. I had no idea you worked so late on a Sunday evening.'

'Normally not,' crackled the voice on the line, 'but for you, yes!'

'I like to hear you talk like that, Wedekind,' replied the detective, 'but I imagine this is more than a courtesy call?'

'No, but what I'm about to say will please you anyway. Listen carefully.'

Owen listened in silence, a broad smile gradually spreading across his face. Then he muttered:

'You're sure? Absolutely sure?'

'I couldn't be more sure. We have three witnesses, two of whom are prepared to swear to it. Allow me to congratulate you. You hit the bull's-eye, with your intuition.'

'Intuition, if you will,' growled Owen. 'It was quite logical to think that it would be in a hotel that... In fact, where was it? In the area I indicated? Yes? Well, then, you see....'

'I was talking about the name, Burns, the name of the hotel... It wasn't the name of a bird, as you had supposed, but close enough... I'll leave you to be the judge. Listen....'

After Owen hung up he stood motionless for a few moments, his hand still on the instrument. Strange thoughts were whirling in his mind. Up until then, he had convinced himself that his astonishing deductive faculties alone had solved the mystery. But now....

He shook himself and picked up the phone once more and asked the operator to connect him to a number in the Cotswolds. Shortly thereafter, he heard a familiar voice.

'Achilles, my dear old friend, how are you? ... Very well, thank you... I'm hoping you can find time to free yourself for twenty-four hours in the days to come... Why?... For the last act, of course!... Yes, yes, the case of the White Lady has finally been solved!'

## 23

### Further talk of the suitcase

*Achilles Stock's account (continued)*

*November 12*

What intrigued me the most was the suitcase Owen was carrying with him. He had briefed me about the latest developments in the case, but had obstinately refused to reveal its contents. It was made of buffalo leather and was over three feet wide, yet hardly seemed to weigh anything. Shaking it, one could detect the presence of light objects, such as paper and perhaps feathers.

If the afternoon was gloomy, the atmosphere in the salon of Buckworth Manor was positively sepulchral. The Richards clan resembled a group of hostile and anxious shadows. Miss Lethia Seagrave, too, seemed anxious, but not so much as the others. Facing them were no less than four representatives of law and order: Inspector Lewis, Owen Burns, myself, and above all Superintendent Wedekind, quite intimidating with his walrus moustache, which gave him the appearance of a primitive brute.

After a weighty silence, Owen began.

'First of all, ladies and gentlemen, I must ask if there are any firearms in the house?'

Following surprised looks and furtive consultation, they agreed that the deceased owned two hunting rifles and two handguns.

'Let's leave the rifles,' continued Owen, 'they're too cumbersome. Do you know where the handguns are located?'

Once again, Ann, Margot and Esther were unanimous: they were in the deceased's study; one in a drawer and the other on a shelf.

'Very well, ladies. I'd be obliged if all three of you would go to find them. Or at least two of you together.'

Ann and Margot left the room. When they reappeared after five minutes Margot, brandishing a revolver, declared:

'We could only find this. The other seems to have disappeared.'

'Was it also a revolver, like this one?'

'No. It was an automatic pistol, black and smaller than this. I couldn't tell you the make. But it's still strange that it's missing.'

'Strange or not,' exclaimed Ann, 'I don't see the relevance, Mr. Burns. Would you be good enough to explain?'

Spinning the barrel of the revolver, Owen replied:

'Willingly. It's true that nobody was hit by a bullet, as we all know. But minuscule amounts of burnt powder were found in your father's hair. We combed the area around the tree under which he was found, but in vain. If you had been able to produce both weapons, I might have been inclined to discard my theory. But now there's a missing pistol... I can understand the murderer's calculation: carefully cleaning the weapon after use—a weapon which has supposedly not been used for eons—would be guaranteed to cause suspicion. Better then to make it disappear. And we don't even need to waste time looking for it: its very absence is proof enough of its use. As for the one I'm holding, it's clear that it hasn't been used for some time. What do you think, Wedekind?'

The superintendent took the weapon and examined it with an expert eye:

'A beautiful weapon... a Webley Mark 1... Almost a collector's piece. No smell of powder. No recent cleaning... I can confirm, no recent use.'

'I don't understand what you're talking about, gentlemen,' said Ann, fuming.

'We'll get back to that later,' replied Owen. 'And things will be a lot clearer, I can assure you. Getting back to the White Lady, whom we now know cannot be Miss Seagrave. Which changes everything, in so many ways. Most of all, it means that she's probably hiding under this roof, and therefore is here amongst us right now. Before going further in that direction I have to tell you that we have also been considering, quite seriously, the theory of revenge on the part of one of the children of Samuel Ziegler—an old enemy of Sir Matthew —who may well have infiltrated here like a fox in a henhouse.'

'And who is amongst us?' asked Vivian in astonishment. 'And even one of us? Is that what we are meant to understand?'

'Yes, particularly given that the ages roughly correspond. But let me put your minds at ease. Everyone has been eliminated. Or almost everyone. There remain two possible suspects, even though very unlikely, it must be said.'

'And who are they?' asked Vivian sharply.

'Why, you, madam. Your personal history is so tortuous it's impossible to follow.'

'So I'm this Ziegler's daughter? I don't even know her... What did she do?'

'When last heard from she was a prostitute in the port of Hamburg. But your similarity to her is limited to her age. And we assume that your late husband would have recognised you if that were the case.'

'You're too kind, Mr. Burns. And who is the other?'

Owen turned to look at John Peel.

'Me?' exclaimed the other, more amused than surprised.

'Yes, you, major. And it might even be a case of double substitution. The Ziegler son, who disappeared in a shipwreck at the time, could well have passed himself off as the man who miraculously escaped from the Afghan rebels, before assuming the identity of Major John Peel.'

'But that's grotesque. It's too far-fetched.'

'And you don't think I'd have noticed?' asked Margot mockingly.

'Of course. But we can't neglect any hypothesis, and you must admit that your husband's extraordinary story does invite some suspicion. That said, we can pursue more plausible theories. If we dismiss the idea of revenge, that leaves the pursuit of the inheritance. We already saw last time that the starting point for this whole affair was Sir Matthew's nightmare, so we won't revisit that except to say that the murderer had established their strategy: frighten Sir Matthew by repeated interventions by the White Lady, in order to weaken him for the fatal blow, where he literally died of fear.

'Who is the murderer? And their possible accomplice? For it seems clear that they could not have operated alone on some of the occasions. We shall attempt to answer by taking the facts in chronological order, and trying to rule out the most promising candidates, so to speak.

'Regarding Sir Matthew's nightmare, it's obvious that the murderer knew what was happening and must also have read Miss Seagrave's automatic writings, before making them disappear temporarily.

'Next there was the death of little Harry at the pond. In my view, the purpose of this event, the only one not to have occurred inside the property, was to reinforce the legend of the White Lady and her deadly power—consistent with Miss Seagrave's writings—and, above all, to frighten Sir Matthew, as if death were about to pay him a visit.

'On that subject, Lady Richards, do you still stand by your story of a rendezvous arranged by the highly improbable Moog?'

'Er, yes,' replied Vivian, caught off guard.

'Well, I think you're lying. First of all, because we've been unable to find any trace of any Andrew Moog. And secondly, I have good reason to believe that the message you received must have been far more compromising for you. On the other hand, if you did play the role of the White Lady that night, it's not clear why you would have shown yourself at the inn.'

Vivian forced a smile.

'Thank you for coming to my defence, Mr. Burns.'

'You just won a point. Hang on to it, because there's a chance you may lose several others later.

'The tragic event at the pond is undoubtedly the most harrowing of all. It was nothing less than Death coming to claim a victim following an accidental poisoning. But taken out of its strange context—a context to which I myself was sensitive for a time—the story does not hold up to rigorous analysis, even taking into account the testimony of Harry's two friends. The idea that he dropped dead as soon as the white hand of the apparition touched him is quite inconceivable. What most surprised me, because of its unlikelihood, is that the lad started to graze grass like a sheep, or more precisely started to chew twigs of hemlock. And that as the result of a dare which he himself had slyly provoked. In short, our little Harry was an accomplice to the scheme, presented to him as a practical joke he could play on his friends. Needless to say, he was unaware of its fatal outcome. The "joke" must have been rehearsed with the "White Lady" that same afternoon, after he'd discovered the fox caught in the trap. Everything happened as we know, up to the point Jack and Billy became alarmed and moved away. That's when our "White Lady" appeared, to "cure" Harry according to the plan. Even though he had spat the twigs out, he couldn't take the risk and needed to swallow the antidote, no matter how unpleasant it tasted. At least, that's what she told him. But what she made him drink, as she stroked his neck with her delicate white hand, wasn't an antidote. On the contrary, it was a hemlock concentrate that she had prepared, along with a few crushed berries from the plant which would be found in his stomach. I can imagine the soothing voice of the enchantress: "It will be painful for a few moments, but it's necessary... Don't move... Lie down."

'And half-an-hour later, Harry was dead, poisoned, exactly as described by Jack and Billy. A Machiavellian murder, certainly, but remarkable from the artistic point of view.'

It was as if an icy wind had blown through the salon. Then Vivian exclaimed:

'It's odious! I could never have done that!'

'Let's take a look at what happened after that,' continued Owen without further comment. 'One night, almost exactly a month ago, our White Lady caused panic in the household. She first made an appearance in Sir Matthew's bedroom, where you happened to be as well, Lady Richards. Your husband hardly saw her and you proceeded to blind him with the bedside lamp, on the pretext of protecting him from the female monster, whilst you, on the other hand, saw her perfectly and described her in astonishing detail, including her face. Given that I was already beginning to suspect collusion that night, I postulated that the apparition might in fact be your accomplice, dressed up in a bed sheet. And then, purely by chance, the lamp was dropped on the floor and the room was plunged into darkness. But you waited an awfully long time before crying out. A long enough time for your accomplice to get rid of the sheet, return discreetly to their bed, and pretend to awake with a start at the sound. The fuses blew shortly thereafter, which is easy to do from any outlet, as I explained previously. In the ensuing panic you returned to your husband, who was in bad shape in his bedroom, to frighten him a second time and possibly in the hope of finishing him off. In the half-light it was easy for you to put on a mask and remove your dressing gown to appear in your nightgown. It was all made easier because you were supposedly, according to several accounts, inspecting the attic with Peter. The same Peter who confirmed you were behind him as he came down the stairs at the very same moment that the major saw the "White Lady" in the corridor at a point level with the landing. That "White Lady" was obviously you, who then went downstairs to evade your pursuers. When the light came back on and, seeing the front door open—it had actually been opened previously—it was assumed that the "White Lady" had fled outside and that she had come from the village, in other words reinforcing the suspicion about Miss Seagrave. I may add that, according to such a hypothesis, your accomplice would be Peter Corsham.'

'What?' howled Ann, her cheeks red with anger. 'You're accusing my husband of—.'

Owen made a soothing gesture.

'As I said, it's just a hypothesis. Other combinations could be envisaged with other actors. In any case, it's clear that an accomplice was necessary. Nevertheless, Lady Richards, your extremely precise description of the White Lady is very suspicious, so I'm going to withdraw the point I awarded you before. As for you, Mr. Corsham, you lose one. Let us proceed to the next act.

'Less than two weeks later, our two accomplices are at work again. This time, it's to deliver the final blow. The arrangements are less complicated than for the previous event, but still carefully prepared. The window was wide open to the cold, a candle was lit to provide the right lighting, and sheets and covers were delicately removed. To cap it all, Sir Matthew's pyjama top was unbuttoned so that his chest would be exposed during what followed. For her part the White Lady had to make a slight sacrifice in order for her hands to be at the right temperature, that is to say glacial, either by simply exposing them to the night cold or by soaking them in cold water. In neither case would it be an agreeable experience, but it was well worth the candle, so to speak! Then she put on her mask, no doubt a very pretty one, but henceforth synonymous with death. One can imagine Sir Matthew's reaction when, awakened by the cold, he saw the apparition. And the terrible shock he felt when the nightmarish creature suddenly placed her frozen hands on his chest. The two accomplices believed that they had finally achieved their goal, but they left the window wide open to be doubly sure. And perhaps to suggest the intruder's escape route, with the added detail of the crow's feather. Which poses the question: who amongst you had the opportunity to procure it?'

After those present had exchanged suspicious looks, Owen continued:

'From what I've been told, only Peter Corsham had visited Miss

Seagrave, and that for a reading of the cards.'

In a falsely apologetic tone, he added:

'I'm sorry, Mr. Corsham, but you lose another point. Which makes two, if my calculations are correct.

'Unfortunately—or fortunately, depending on your point of view—Sir Matthew recovered from the attack, which should theoretically have been his last. The next time they had to be absolutely sure. And at the same time implicate Miss Seagrave, which explains the rendezvous message inviting her to the scene of the crime—an attempt which failed, as I explained last time. They had to find a new way, given that frightening him with a white mask hadn't worked so far. I've found examples of the method used in police annals, but perhaps they invented it themselves. It doesn't really matter. This is how it worked. During his customary walk in the park, Sir Matthew is accosted by a hooded intruder who threatens him with a gun and ties him to a tree with his hands behind his back, protected by a scarf in order to leave no marks. He gags Sir Matthew as well, because he needs to leave him alone for a few moments and cannot risk him calling out. When he returns, he's brandishing a revolver.'

Owen stopped and picked up the weapon found in the dead man's study.

'This one, of course,' he said, spinning the barrel and pulling the trigger each time it stopped. 'Maybe he talked about the White Lady and her imminent arrival. In any case, he made it clear they were going to play Russian roulette. The gun was pressed against Sir Matthew's forehead and at regular intervals he heard a terrifying click echo in his skull, up to the point a loud detonation was heard. It didn't come from the revolver, which wasn't loaded, but from the pistol—the one which has so conveniently disappeared. And it's the latter which, angled differently, but still close to the unfortunate victim's head, left the powder residue on his hair. It's already enough to make a healthy man faint. For Sir Matthew, subject to frequent heart attacks, it proved fatal.'

'That's utterly grotesque!' exclaimed Vivian. 'You're making it up. Let me remind you that no one, absolutely no one heard the loud detonation you describe.'

Turning to John Peel, Owen asked:

'What do you think, major, from a technical point of view?'

'It's obvious. My father-in-law's heart couldn't take it... As for the rest, I can confirm that we never heard a sound. And I have very acute hearing.'

'Well, now we're going to review everyone's movements that evening.'

He pulled a notebook out of his pocket and began to read out loud:

'Six o'clock. Vivian, Ann, Margot, John and Sir Matthew are in the salon—in other words, here. Sir Matthew goes out for his walk and John goes to the billiard room.

'At a quarter-past six, Peter joins John in the billiard room. Ann leaves the salon and is replaced by Esther.

'At half-past six, Ann returns to the salon, as do John and Peter. Vivian is worried about her husband's absence. A heated quarrel broke out between Vivian and Peter, which ended with Peter leaving, apparently very upset. That was at twenty-to seven or slightly earlier. Shortly after a quarter-to seven it was Vivian's turn to leave, very upset as well, to find her husband. On her way out she slammed the doors behind her so violently, particularly the front door, that the walls shook. Once outside, she immediately saw the White Lady—it was becoming a habit, decidedly!—and went back inside to alert the others. A disorganised search followed, during the course of which Peter joined in, and the body was discovered at around seven o'clock.'

Owen closed the notebook and nodded.

'What emerges from it all is that Margot is the one person who can be ruled out. She never once left the salon. Ann, Esther, John and Peter were each absent for at least a quarter of an hour, time enough to ambush Sir Matthew and tie him to a tree as described. To be frank, it's more like the act of a man. Moving on to the sound of the shot. It's obvious that there's only one noise which could have drowned it out, and that's the door slamming so hard behind Vivian that "the walls shook." Once again I bow to your judgment and experience, major. What do you think?'

John Peel appeared embarrassed.

'It's possible, of course. But the two sounds would have had to coincide perfectly.'

Owen nodded his head with a knowing smile and went slowly over to Peter Corsham. Looking him in the eye, he declared:

'The only one outside at that moment was you. As soon as you left, you went to meet your future victim again, still gagged and tied to the tree. That's when you started your little game of Russian roulette, with one eye on the front door. The light goes on in the entrance hall. That's the signal. The door opens to reveal your accomplice... It's the moment. You shoot with your loaded pistol... Then you remove the victim's bindings and go to mix discreetly with the others.'

'That's absurd,' muttered Peter. 'Any accomplice on the outside could have done it.'

'So you acknowledge the trick of the door slamming?'

'No, I don't acknowledge anything at all. It's all pure speculation.'

'Despite the disappearing pistol? So be it, but I'm obliged to deduct an extra point, and from Lady Richards as well. It's starting to weigh heavily in the balance.'

He turned to his dumbfounded audience:

'Don't you think so?'

He pivoted theatrically, crossed his hands behind his back, and said:

'In that case, let us continue. There are no further acts, but in fact we have skipped one, the very first intervention of the White Lady in the manor in mid-June. I did that deliberately, to spare Mr. Corsham, who would otherwise have had two points deducted at the start, which would not have been very elegant on my part. I have to admit that episode posed a serious problem of chronology and disrupted my reasoning, in the sense that the White Lady made an appearance well before the arrival of Vivian as a secretary. And that was all to the credit of Mr. Corsham, whose master stroke almost makes me want to attribute two points, as much in respect as in admiration. Let us briefly recall the facts. Going out of the house late in order to smoke a cigarette, Mr. Corsham sees the White Lady, who exits by passing miraculously through the wire boundary fence. And there's a witness, namely his own wife. The event is deemed to be the first manifestation chronologically. Which is both true and false.

'Let me explain. What is true is that Ann did see Peter that night, in the company of a woman who quickly disappeared. A woman who wasn't "white," by the way, according to her testimony. Faced with her husband's confused explanations, she suspected he was cheating on her—and she wasn't wrong. I have no proof, but there's every reason to believe that the woman was none other than Vivian—Vivian Marsh at the time—and they were already having an affair. It was only *afterwards*, three months later, just after Sir Matthew's nightmare, that the bit about "the White Lady who spreads the cold and passes through wire fences" was added by Peter. That was very subtle on his part because it also had the effect of clearing him in the eyes of his wife, who had suspected him of adultery: if he hadn't mentioned it at the time, it was because his story was too fantastic to be believed. But obviously, after Sir Matthew's nightmare, it now made sense... And so we have two simple incidents—a nightmare and an embellished story—opportunistically used by our two cunning accomplices. A good part of the preparatory work has been done without the slightest effort!'

Solemnly, Owen turned to Ann:

'You are the best placed, madam, to comment on my observations. I'd like to hear your recollection of events.'

For a moment, Ann sat as still as a statue. Then her composure crumbled and she looked at her husband.

'Peter! Tell me it's not true.'

'Of course not,' he replied, shrugging his shoulders. 'I realise things look black portrayed that way, but I've told the truth, nothing but the truth. And it was only because of your father's dream, which seemed so real, that I was reminded of the bizarre event. It's possible that I embroidered the facts a little, either because of time or mimicry, but the essence is true.'

Ann, now deathly pale, was still not convinced. Pointing to Vivian with a trembling finger, she asked:

'You've never had relations with her? Do you swear it?'

'Yes, my darling, of course.'

'You're very reassuring, Mr. Corsham,' continued Owen. 'It's basically your word against my theory. Nevertheless, I believe I'm right, because in the aftermath you paid a visit to Miss Seagrave, to ask her in particular whether the White Lady would appear again. I find it hard to imagine any soothsayer in such circumstances saying: "No, don't worry. The White Lady will never appear again." Such being the case, you came back to announce, in funereal tones, that something tragic was soon going to occur. Inwardly, though, you were overjoyed. That was the next step in your plan. But your visit had another, more important, purpose—and I'm not talking about the crow's feather that only you could have stolen—to decide whether Miss Seagrave would make an ideal culprit. You decided she would, and so proceeded to the third step: the death of little Harry at the pond.'

'It's insane!' exclaimed Vivian, crimson with anger. 'They're words, just words! Words which you play with for the sole pleasure of hearing yourself speak, tormenting us, moving us around like pieces on a chessboard to test your little combinations. Do we really need this after we've just lived through a dreadful experience?'

'You're very impressive, Mr. Burns,' said Peter, having regained his aplomb. 'But you must recognise that outsiders other than Miss Seagrave—who seems to have been ruled out—could have carried out the plot. Maybe you should look into the Ziegler children more assiduously. What do you think, Inspector Lewis? And you, Superintendent Wedekind?'

The latter appeared hesitant.

'Maybe so... It's true that everything so far has been theoretical, without any palpable proof. Justice likes proof.'

'Ah, proof,' said Owen, hitting his forehead with his hand. 'I was forgetting... Achilles, my good friend, where did you put the suitcase?'

'There, near the sofa,' I replied with alacrity. 'Stay there, I'll bring it over.'

Owen grabbed it, tested its weight and handed it to Vivian, who took it as if it were a hot potato.

Then, finding it to be curiously light, she murmured, with a gleam of hope in her black eyes:

'I think I understand, Mr. Burns. It contains *all the rubbish you've just spouted.*'

'Would it were so, madam, sincerely. But it's not entirely empty. Here, let me show you.'

He opened it, displaying to the stunned onlookers three large peacock feathers, which explained the width of the suitcase.

'Aren't they magnificent?' he asked. 'There's something majestic about them, with their iridescent blue-green colours. I don't know why, but I've always adored peacock feathers since I was a child.'

I was becoming more and more puzzled. Where was my friend

going with this?

'The three peacock feathers,' he repeated. 'Or, rather, *The Peacock Feathers,* a small hostelry in Ramillies Street in the middle of London, comfortable and discreet. There's even a box of matches with a symbol of them with the address. Maybe you've had the opportunity to use one like it?'

Peter Corsham went suddenly pale and Superintendent Wedekind pulled back his jacket to reveal a service pistol.

'And now we come to these two photos,' said Owen, plunging his hand into the suitcase again. 'Two photos of the two of you together, as you can see. I think the one of Mr. Corsham is rather flattering, particularly compared to his current expression. As for you, Lady Richards, it isn't....'

Putting on his most charming smile, Owen continued:

'I find you just as pretty as in real life. I think your beauty has been one of your principal assets throughout your existence. But this time it worked to your disadvantage. Three of the hotel's employees recognised you immediately they saw the picture. There are very few women like you. As for Mr. Corsham, there was some hesitation. But the cheque he wrote during one of your extended stays settled the question. According to the hotel, the two of you were regular customers between June and August. Needless to say, your clandestine affair will weigh heavily against you.'

Wedekind took a step forward and declared solemnly:

'I'm arresting you both in the name of the law for double homicide. Anything you say—.'

'We never killed that child!' screamed Vivian.

'Be quiet,' said Peter angrily. 'Don't say a word. We need to wait for—.'

Two violent slaps reduced him to silence. Then Ann, clutching her hand, collapsed into an armchair, sobbing her heart out.

## 24

### Epilogue

*November 15*

Lost in thought, Owen Burns was walking along Buckworth High Street when he almost collided with a figure emerging from an alleyway. It was none other than Inspector Lewis.

'Burns!' he exclaimed. 'I didn't expect to see you here again after the end of that Richards business. What the devil are you doing here?'

'I could ask you the same thing,' replied Owen with a smile.

The policeman looked back at the house behind him, which was half covered by vegetation, and sighed.

'I was trying to assess the amount of work needed, which I seem to have underestimated. It's the family home, as you know. I'm wondering whether it's worth it. It's a formidable task.'

'Would you like my advice?'

'It would be very welcome.'

'I don't think it's a problem about the size of the job, because you certainly don't lack courage. The real question is whether you really want to stay here.'

'There's no fooling you, is there?' replied the inspector, smiling.

'Personally, I think your place is here, my dear fellow.'

'Really? But in fact you haven't answered my question.'

'Well,' replied Owen hesitantly, 'it's to say goodbye to Miss Seagrave. The circumstances weren't ripe the last time, during the final explanations.'

'She's been out of sorts,' mused Lewis. 'The death of her father affected her greatly. During his burial, she was clearly the most affected.'

'Have you spoken to her since?'

'Barely a few words in passing. I don't think she's forgiven the trick I played on her to get the feather.'

'I'd be surprised. You should go and see her yourself.'

The policeman shrugged his shoulders undecidedly, then exclaimed:

'What a business! I have to say I had my doubts about you at first, Mr. Burns, but you certainly came through in the end, confronting the culprits in masterly fashion the other night. That Peter must be an idiot. He could have waited patiently for his wife to inherit, instead of getting involved in such a complicated plot—with a highly dubious accomplice into the bargain. Was it worth the risk?'

'In my opinion, they weren't planning to stop there. It's almost certain that their next victim would have been Ann. She was the last obstacle to their eternal happiness in unimaginable luxury, and Peter would have collected another part of the fabulous inheritance on the way to paradise.'

'What a diabolical couple! And to think they didn't hesitate to get there over the dead body of a child.'

'I'm not so sure about that,' replied Owen, looking down.

'Ah! I see! Her pathetic protestation of innocence melted your heart!'

'That's true,' smiled Owen. 'It's always regrettable to see such a beautiful creature finish up behind bars, or even at the end of a rope. But perhaps a good lawyer and her ravishing looks will get her a lighter sentence? Be that as it may, Wedekind and I don't envisage charging her for the child's death.'

'Oh? And why is that?'

'First of all, there's already been a verdict of accidental death. Secondly, because it differs significantly from the other interventions of the "White Lady", both in the scene of the crime and the choice of victim. And thirdly, because a clever lawyer would have quickly shone the light on the strange attitude of Lady Richards, signalling her presence in the village by showing herself for half-an-hour just before the incident in question... And an alibi for that period would have sown doubt on everything else.'

The policeman nodded his head:

'That's quite possible, in fact. I hadn't thought about that.'

'And there's something else you haven't thought about either, I'll wager.'

'What's that?'

'You. You could have been a prime suspect.'

'Me?' exclaimed the inspector, his eyes wide in astonishment.

'Why, yes. You could have been the famous vanished son of Ziegler, given your long absence from the village. You had the perfect profile of an unexpected criminal, that of an honest and diligent policeman, and, as such, totally above suspicion.'

'And is that what you thought?'

Owen's smile broadened:

'The idea did occur to me, I must admit, notably after you found the crow's feather. You seemed so sincere, so devoted, so professional, it seemed too good to be true... What can I say? After thirty years in the business, you become cynical. I hope you'll forgive my frankness.'

'Of course,' replied Lewis, highly amused. 'But I've learnt my lesson: I shall be less sincere and devoted the next time!'

After a friendly handshake, the two men went their separate ways.

Shortly afterwards Owen found himself in the company of Lethia and her usual circle of companions. One of the cats was in her lap, purring contentedly.

'I was expecting you, Mr. Burns,' she said mischievously.

'Your intuition, I presume?'

'You could call it that.'

'In fact that's exactly what I wanted to talk about: your famous intuitions. And to tell you that you almost fooled me the last time. To the point that I was firmly convinced that it was I who had discovered the culprits' nest from subtle inferences. And to tell myself that it was logical that Peter and Vivian were already lovers before her marriage to Sir Matthew, so it was probable that they occasionally met in a hotel. I had assiduously developed that hypothesis by limiting the field of investigation to an imaginary line from Paddington Station to Peter's office in Wardour Street, via the Oxford Circus underground. In particular the last section, which he would have covered on foot. I assumed he would choose a hotel on that last leg and explored the possibility of payment by cheque. So you see, I'd almost convinced myself that everything had been my idea and you had merely contributed a few insignificant items to help me concentrate. But then there was that third card, with the birds, where you had emphasised: "lots of feathers"!'

Owen shook his head smilingly, before adding:

'But that was one detail too many. Particularly when I discovered that your office in Oxford Street was a stone's throw from *The Peacock Feathers*. That aside, you've been very clever in your choice of words. In fact, I believe you know your cards so well that you are able to suggest whatever you want by a simple association of ideas. The words "hate" and "cabin" don't evoke much, any more than "jealousy" or "building". But with "hotel" and "clandestine affairs", the image of two lovers meeting secretly springs immediately to mind. And I thought that it was I who had made the connection... Very clever. A brilliant exercise in mental manipulation.'

'You're no slouch in that department yourself, Mr. Burns.'

'Perhaps. Even though I feel I can't hold a candle to you. That said, my visit to you was rich in information: it made me realise that you were well aware of Peter and Vivian's affair. Either you guessed it or, more likely, you saw Peter by accident one day, going into that hotel with a pretty woman who was not his wife.'

Lethia, with an enigmatic smile, continued to caress her cat.

After a short pause, Owen changed the subject:

'I ran into Inspector Lewis on my way here. He saw you at the burial and said you were quite overcome.'

'Is that surprising?'

'A little, given that, in your own words, you saw your father as two different men. One good, the other bad.'

'You must have realised the simple reason: I loved him because he was my father, and I bore him a grudge for having abandoned me and my mother.'

'Your mother, who had judiciously given you the name Lethia, "the forgotten" in Greek. A very rare one, recalling the famous river of forgetfulness, which you refer to on the plaque of your shop.'

'Nothing escapes your eagle eye, Mr. Burns. I'm impressed.'

'But, in the end, your father had not forgotten you, either morally or financially, in his will. You were the only one to whom he left a personal letter, and I believe it changed your point of view about him. To a very great extent.'

Lethia nodded and swallowed hard.

'That's true. I realised how much he loved me and how he had never really "forgotten" me. And how much he regretted the stupid social conventions which had erected a barrier against us, a barrier which had never existed in his heart. He also told me how much he had loved my mother and....'

She broke out in tears.

'I understand.'

'No, you can never understand,' she sobbed.

'Oh, but yes. And I can even tell you that your failure to appreciate him will haunt you to your final breath.'

She looked at him in sudden surprise.

'I come back to the fact that you've known about Peter and Vivian's adulterous relationship for a long time. That opened my eyes in many respects and prompted me to ask myself certain questions, notably about Vivian's culpability in the death at the pond... I don't think it was she who played the role of the White Lady. I think it was you.'

In the silence that followed, Owen lit a cigarette and watched the smoke rings thoughtfully as they rose to the ceiling. Then he continued:

'It's only a hypothesis, because I can't prove it, but I do want to develop it from a theoretical point of view. Besides, I've always felt that, from a psychological standpoint, you wouldn't have the slightest problem sacrificing and poisoning that little troublemaker Harry. You detested him to the point of hating him for his unpardonable crime in your eyes: the torture of animals. You even announced your motive in my presence when you described what he did to your cat, thinking that such a display of frankness on your part would allay suspicion. Or maybe you preferred to tell me before I learnt it from someone else? You were also in a much better position than Vivian to trick him and manipulate him, having feigned reconciliation with him. Not to mention the deadly hemlock preparation, which I imagine your knowledge of herbs placed you in a far better position to prepare. Finally, there's the secret message sent to Vivian, to arrange a meeting on the fatal night. Your objective was to get her out of the manor, where she might have had an alibi, and get her closer to the pond so that she would be suspected of playing the part of the White Lady in front of the children. I'm willing to bet the message contained an allusion to her affair with Peter. Which she obviously couldn't talk about, and which forced her to invent a feeble excuse about an imaginary Andrew Moog.'

'And I dreamt up that elaborate comedy just to get rid of that wretch? If that's what I'd wanted, there were dozens of simpler ways.'

'Certainly. But it wasn't just about getting rid of Harry. Let's look more closely at the situation you found yourself in at that moment, still hypothetically, of course. You knew Peter and Vivian were lovers. You suspected that the two of them coveted the inheritance from your father. You knew that the first visit of the White Lady to the manor was purely imaginary, following his nightmare. You knew that the nightmare was a direct result of the book he'd borrowed from you. Even if you hadn't read it yourself—which I strongly doubt— you knew what it was about. The story about the vengeful White Lady, the White Lady you admired, came undoubtedly from you. Or a fantasised version, shall we say. And, starting from there, you must have readily understood that Peter had blatantly lied when he embellished at a later date the episode of the unknown woman seen near the fountain. At that stage, then, you had every reason to believe that it wouldn't be long before the two lovers took action and created another supposed manifestation of the White Lady....

'But then, lo and behold! Peter comes to visit you! I was not, alas! present, but I can easily imagine the meeting, a veritable chess match between two thought manipulators. On the one hand Peter, sizing you up with a view to making you the culprit; and on the other, you, perfectly aware of his plans. And, contrary to what he thought when he left, it was you who had completely manipulated him. I'm willing to bet that you encouraged him through an adroit drawing of cards. The diabolical couple were preparing to get their hands on your father's inheritance, or a good part of it, and you couldn't let that happen. Your idea was to let them proceed almost to the end, before exposing them. They were in your hands. You could denounce them at any time, by revealing their frequent visits to *The Peacock Feathers*, which would have been devastating for them. One might wonder why you didn't denounce them earlier....

'Before answering that question, I want to get back to Harry's death. You wouldn't have killed him just for personal revenge, particularly since the incident, chronologically speaking, occurred shortly after Peter's visit, during which you announced that the White Lady would strike again soon. You committed the crime to follow other events, to help the diabolical couple, guiding them, encouraging them... Obviously Vivian and Peter must have been very surprised by the event, which must have looked like a gift from heaven. Very intriguing, but why worry if it served their ends?... And they followed in turn.

'And all this time you were following the course of the affair, at home, in comfort. I don't say peacefully, because you knew you were a suspect and that your adversaries were plotting to pin everything on you. That was what allowed you to react swiftly, on the night of your father's murder, when they tried to entrap you with the anonymous message about a rendezvous at the manor. Once you had confirmed the deception by going there early, you immediately sought refuge with the Nicholls to give yourself an alibi. But you weren't running any risk, because at any time you could have pulled the trump card of *The Peacock Feathers* out of your sleeve.

'I confess that this criminal to-and-fro—each party operating in the shadows, whilst advancing one of its chess pieces—had me quite puzzled. In fact, I can't remember such a situation in my long career as an investigator. And there remains the troubling question of your passivity, the fact that you didn't warn your father about the plot being hatched against him by the lovers. One word from you, at any time, could have saved him, but you didn't do it. Why?

'I imagine you thought about it for a long time. You weighed your blood ties against the "crimes" you thought he had committed. The good man on one side and the bad one on the other. Because I don't think it was to hasten the due date of your part of the inheritance. Eventually you made the decision we know. But after the posthumous letter you realised you had been mistaken about him. Your profound grief is the proof.'

There was a long silence. Owen faced Lethia's impenetrable gaze.

'All of that is theoretical, Mr. Burns,' she said eventually. 'You're as adept with words and ideas as I am with cards... And if we associate cards with ideas, your theory could well be a house of cards, don't you think?'

'Quite so. And I understand the allusion: a fragile edifice which can be blown over. Particularly since I admit I have no proof and little chance of finding any, should I care to try. For, in practice, you didn't do anything but indulge in psychological manoeuvres, with the exception of the intervention of the White Lady at the pond. As for your father, I fear his memory will forever haunt you, and each time you visit his grave you will see *"The eye which was in the tomb and regarded Cain"*.'

'Victor Hugo.'

'Correct. And before my house of cards collapses—for the area is very windy, I fear—I have a thought for the little companions you have collected and cared for. It would distress me to see them abandoned to their fate. You have nurtured them and will continue to do so, and that probably outweighs any hypothetical misdeeds.'

The young woman's big brown eyes shone with increased intensity.

'I knew you were a friend, Mr. Burns. I knew at our first meeting.'

Owen held the soothsayer's eye:

'I can resist anything, Miss Seagrave, except the mysterious gaze of a cat.'

Lethia sat for a long time without moving, then declared in a changed voice:

'Speaking of which, I have a small problem. Our family has just got bigger. I accepted three little orphans from a neighbouring farm. Three adorable kittens. I've managed to find a home for two of them, but there's one left. Do you know someone who might be interested?'

Owen had never doubted that Lethia was a strange woman, very different from the others. But the astonishing ease with which she could change the subject, in such instants, left him almost speechless. After a moment's thought, he nodded in agreement.

'Yes. I'm thinking of Inspector Lewis. I think he would make a good father for the kitten, amongst others....'

THE END

CPSIA information can be obtained
at www.ICGtesting.com
Printed in the USA
LVHW052350300820
664592LV00017B/2270

SEP 03 2020